I0715836

ALSO BY ANNE RENWICK

FLIGHT OF THE SCARAB

AN ELEMENTAL WEB TALE

ANNE RENWICK

Publisher's Note: This is a work of fiction. Names, characters, places, and incidents are a product of the author's imagination. Locales and public names are sometimes used for atmospheric purposes. Any resemblance to actual people, living or dead, or to businesses, companies, events, institutions, or locales is completely coincidental.

Flight of the Scarab/ Anne Renwick. — 1st ed.

ISBN 978-1-948359-48-1

Cover design by James T. Egan of Bookfly Design.

Edited by Sandra Sookoo.

To Donald Dodson

THANK YOU TO...

Donald Dodson whose offhand comment about mushroom insects was the eureka moment the story rattling around in my head needed to stop shape-shifting and take its final form.

Sandra Sookoo, my wonderful editor who mercilessly ferrets out weaknesses and sets my work on a better course.

My husband who puts up with all my strangeness as he patiently waits for my next book to take shape.

My mom and dad who instilled in me a love of both reading and travel.

Mr. Fox and his red pen.

CHAPTER ONE

The Monocled Raven
London
June 1885

Reed Harlowe fell forward onto the bar, propped himself up upon his elbows and produced an irreverent grin. "Hear me out."

Julia Marston rolled her eyes and set aside the glass she was drying. Once, her pub had been filled with lively chatter and boisterous laughter. Evenings involved toasts with clinking glasses, music and song. And the occasional good-natured argument over a pint of ale. Now, her family's pub was half empty. Sounds were reduced to the hiss of gas lamps, a faint clatter of dishes and soft murmurs of low-pitched conversations.

Most of her staff had left as well. She alone stood ready

to serve patrons a pint. Not that there were many. She'd sent the bored cook home an hour past.

"What nonsense is it this time?" At best Harlowe was a nuisance. At worst, a source of marital discord. Why her husband tolerated his presence—as student or as employee—baffled her. Half the time, Marston looked ready to throttle the man. Especially of late. Perhaps it was a case of 'keep your enemies close'?

Either way, the two men were the source of all her problems.

The pub, or rather the business it now fronted, was not turning the profit her husband expected. Or so she surmised. Marston had rebuffed her every inquiry. His mood could be likened to a gathering of overhead storm clouds. Lightning was bound to strike soon. Precisely where, when or who? Impossible to predict. But she didn't wish to be caught standing in the open when the inevitable occurred.

"If someone crossed yeast with a fluorescent green jelly-fish," Harlowe began, "how much would such a will-o'-the-wisp yeast be worth to you if it could be used to produce a glow-in-the-dark beer?"

Her ears pricked as he spoke, wishing she could believe he did more than tease. She refused to take the bait. Every idea that fell from his lips in the guise of friendship focused on profit over scientific rigor.

Every single time.

Her eyes narrowed. She was tired of the constant battle to refute the increasingly nonsensical proposals he dropped before her like a cat with a dead mouse.

Worse, it was a constant reminder that some dreams must be abandoned. Her marriage was no longer even tolerable, making escape the best option. If only she could decide how.

Harlowe knew how much she valued her family's pub, of her all-but-abandoned plans to improve and expand their offerings. He also knew that her marriage contract placed control of The Monocled Raven completely in her husband's hands. A man who ignored her every suggestion to draw in new customers.

Rejections that had mystified her at first. Until she'd opened a crate in the back storeroom looking for a wheel of Stilton cheese and instead discovered a collection of Egyptian antiquities.

Suddenly everything made sense. The shift in clientele. The perfectly average, uninspired food and drink her husband insisted they serve. After all, gastronomic innovation would draw attention, an undesirable trait when one wished to keep a low profile.

Even worse, Harlowe was deeply embedded in Marston's questionable enterprise, helping to identify and entice buyers into the pub which primarily served as a façade for his backroom deals. A business which had functioned smoothly until a few months ago. There'd been some kind of heated exchange that passed between them over a pub table. Eyes narrow, jawlines tight and hard, their words pitched low. Papers had changed hands. And Harlowe had carted a straw bee skep and other beekeeping essentials up the stairs, nestling his latest project among her small rooftop garden.

Determined to produce his own honey this month, he'd brought another straw skep into her kitchen today, promising to carry it to the rooftop later.

Though civil ever since, Harlowe's old friends—unshaven, torc-wearing and mead-drinking—reappeared, joining him at a table far from where Marston gathered with his high society-minded customers.

Alas, much as she'd hoped, they'd not yet parted ways.

Which made the constant stream of bizarre ideas Harlowe carefully sculpted to suit her interests both point-less and exasperating. Any sort of friendship they'd once shared was long past its expiration date. But until her husband made a clear break, she endeavored to endure Harlowe's company when he hung about the bar, soliciting her attention. Still, while she managed polite, she'd rather eat the mold off two-week-old bread than stand here pretending to think his "ideas" valid.

Why wouldn't he leave her alone?

Instead, he sat attentive, awaiting her answer.

"How much would it be worth?" She set down a final glass, tossed aside the damp dish towel. "Not so much as a single shilling." Her inhale fought against reluctant ribs. Her reply passed over clenched teeth. "Such cross-kingdom chimeras are nothing but far-fetched fantasies."

Perhaps someday science would find a way to lift a single hereditary trait from one organism and transfer it into another, but she doubted the code would be unlocked anytime soon.

"It made me think of you when I heard of such an idea. Green glowing beer." Oblivious to her discomfort—or uncaring—he lifted a casual shoulder. Beneath the open collar of his shirt, a torc flashed silver around his neck. He'd taken to wearing the item recently, another way to insert himself among his scruffy friends. "Just so you know I'm always looking out for you."

Harlowe might be indifferent to the sharp, cold needles of her husband's stare. She, however, was not. Ever jealous, Marston envied anyone who possessed more than him. Academic influence. Personal wealth. Youthful vigor.

The last trait was impossible to maintain as time passed during the acquisition of the former two. Gray hairs. Reading glasses. A loosening of skin at the jowls. She'd caught him scowling at his image in the mirror more than once. And at Harlowe who, in his prime, was a clear favorite with their female customers. As such, Marston disapproved of their every interaction, resentful of his own hand-picked protégé.

An imagined threat, her husband's worry about displacement. Especially as Harlowe rarely finished anything, including academic degrees or relationships. The word "commitment" was not in his vocabulary and he preferred to direct his efforts at projects that promised overnight success.

Still, of late her husband's mood swirled about like a thick fog, clouding their every interaction and creating a tense atmosphere of jealousy.

There was little she could do to assuage her husband's prickly ego on this point. Well, little she cared to do, in any case. Their arrangement was one of convenience, of business. And she had nothing of which to be ashamed. Ever since speaking her vows, her behavior had been beyond reproach.

"Julia?" Harlowe always demanded a response. "I know how much you wished to keep your mother's dream alive."

A busier pub would provide her with excuses to walk away, to turn her back on him and attend to other customers. But foot traffic tonight was at an all-time low.

"Plans change all the time." A vague answer she hoped would convince him to return to his more interesting table companions.

As a young woman, her mother had arrived from Latvia with nothing save a paper packet of yeast and her ancestors' knowledge of beer brewing. Skills she'd leveraged to lift herself out of poverty. While Julia's sisters were interested only in leaving trade behind, Julia had begged her mother to teach her the "stone beer" brewing process, where hot rocks were added to beer mixtures in wooden casks, a process used when large metal kettles were expensive and scarce. It produced a lightly acidic and smokey beer and, upon occasion, Julia would make a cask or two, serving it under the name *Senču*, Latvian for ancestor.

Harlowe's solicitous oversight had once been amusing. For about a month. As a female pursuing Mesopotamian studies within the walls of the British Museum, she'd certainly encountered her share of male attention, both positive and negative. Rarely had anyone of academic stature evaluated her research without first factoring in the length of her skirts, the circumference of her waist, the fullness of her bodice and then, finally, her marital status.

Once she'd married Angus Marston, professor of Egyptology, a man of considerable power in his spheres of influence, they became more deferential—a blessing—yet more reluctant to engage in cooperative work—a curse. All told, the balance had tipped against her.

Her mistake, or as her father would call it, salvation, had been knocking on Professor Marston's office door. An innocent request for a letter of introduction to Georg Ebers, German Egyptologist and owner of a renowned medical papyrus reputed to have recorded a number of ancient remedies involving bread and beer.

From the very moment Marston laid eyes upon her, a certain acquisitiveness had brightened his visage. She'd been granted her letter of introduction, but at a steep price.

The very memory left a sour taste in her mouth.

Now here she was, struggling to maintain equilibrium while juggling three glass balls. A husband. The pub. Her Mesopotamian studies. A single wrong move and one—if not all three—was bound to slip from her grasp and shatter upon the floor. If only the three weren't so inextricably linked, she'd be tempted to drop the first and pretend shock.

She poured Harlowe's preferred drink, mead, into an old, abused pewter tankard. Set it down upon the time-worn wood. Shoved a plate of potted kraken on toast toward him and issued a blunt, direct order. "Chitinous hooks removed. Now scoot. Your overlord disapproves of your attentions."

Harlowe barked a loud laugh of the variety that drew eyes. "Overlord." He shook his head, making not the slightest effort to rise from his barstool. Instead, his voice dropped. "There's a rumor, my dearest mycophile, that you've revived past interests in chasing after folkloric fungi."

For the briefest of moments, her breath froze in her lungs.

True, she did cultivate a few mushrooms in a terrarium, one tucked into the dark recesses of the kitchen. But they were strictly culinary. No varieties could be called magical, medicinal or hallucinogenic. She'd been careful, so very careful. Such fungi could have no safe place inside a British pub.

Was her secret out? Was Marston aware? Not questions she dared ask. She'd confided her interest in folklore to Harlowe long ago when she'd thought their friendship would endure. So much for promises of secrecy. Better to ignore the implied question and instead address his inadvisable overfamiliarity. She forced her lips into a purse of disapproval and all but threw her dishtowel at him. "One of these days, Marston is going to wring your neck for spouting such endearments."

"Not mine." His grin widened. "Leyburn's perhaps. If the traitor ever dares show his face." His voice dropped. "Speaking of, have you heard from him?"

From the frying pan into the fire.

The details of the accusations against Graham Leyburn had been kept from her, but she found it impossible to believe he'd steal from the British Museum. Now, if someone had made the same claim against Harlowe, such allegations might have merit.

Once the three of them—as young, starry-eyed students whose studies had converged upon Egypt—had been fast friends. Or so she'd believed. There had been a few short blissful months of camaraderie before everything had gone sideways.

A knock upon Marston's door. A shocking marriage proposal.

Graham's suggestive wink. An ill-advised, brief *affaire de coeur*.

Regretful decisions and her world upturned.

Her—past—relationship with Graham was not a topic for discussion. Not here. Not anywhere.

"No." She put a sharp bite into her one-word answer. Not a lie.

Nothing written. Nothing direct. Not the slightest communication to indicate they'd ever shared more than a casual friendship. A tangential offer voiced in an undertone by an interested party who identified himself as Mr. Black didn't count. An offer she'd never share with anyone, let alone Harlowe, a man of questionable loyalties. Still, it appeared a whisper or two had reached his ear by grapevine. Academics would gossip among themselves.

An exit from her unhappy existence was on offer, a bribe to turn traitor. At first, she'd refused. But the possibility of escaping the circle of her husband's influence called to her, a beckoning siren. Marston no longer showed any interest in visiting her bed. Perhaps he'd be happy to loose her leash, to let her set up a small household in Oxford?

Which meant magic and mushrooms were once again very much on the menu. But did she dare allow Harlowe to see her interest? There was always a price for accepting help from him. Akin to following foxfire into a dark swamp. All but destined to end badly.

She nudged the plate of kraken. "Your toast grows cold."

"So it does." He lifted the plate and, reaching for the tankard, spoke from the corner of his mouth. "Under a tall pine tree not too far from the Egyptian Avenue, there's a glowing fairy ring in Highgate Cemetery. I've heard whispers about nighttime dances…"

As he returned to his scruffy friends, she stared after him, poleaxed. Not at his suggestion that mythological creatures might well exist, but that there was a fairy circle in Highgate Cemetery.

Exciting news all on its own. But the possibility of pinemushrooms? That particular detail held much allure. *Tricholoma.* An edible mycorrhizal mushroom prized for its complex odor—fruity and spicy, but also musty—but primarily for its rumored health benefits. A mushroom that could be fermented to produce a mildly alcoholic beverage.

Damn him. Her weakness for all things yeast was well known. Her thesis did, after all, focus upon the role of beer and bread in early Egyptian and Mesopotamian civilizations. What she kept closer was her fascination with all things fermentable, specifically as applied to traditional foods. She could count on one hand the number of people who knew of her interest in folklore that could be tied to fungi.

A pine-mushroom fairy ring in London.

The perfect lure.

Not that she had any business running off to a cemetery, collecting mushrooms to set up in the stillroom. Nothing would come of it. Not unless she was prepared to commit to Oxford.

Was she?

With effort, she forced her arm to move, pushed a damp cloth across the bar top, wiping away spills. Her skin tingled, both an energizing and agitating sensation. Marston's misplaced jealousy was suffocating. And her academic work was suffering. If she didn't agree to help the Queen's agents, would she be stuck in this miserable downward spiral, her life contracting until it was no larger than a black speck of mold on a discarded heel of bread, the onset of inevitable, all-encompassing decay?

There was no help for it. She would answer Mr. Black's questions, provide him with lists of items that passed through the back room and the names of customers who carted it away. All in hopes he was as good as his word, that a new life awaited her in the history department of Oxford.

"Julia?" Marston's hand cupped her elbow.

"Yes?" She stiffened. Lost in thought, she'd missed his approach.

Icy gray eyes sparked with a light she'd not witnessed since their wedding day. Her stomach clenched. So much for hoping they'd settled into a mere business partnership, if an uneasy one.

They occupied separate rooms above the pub—and he'd not visited her bed for months. A relief, given his frustrated, angry efforts. Efforts that had never managed to end in consummation. Not that she'd dare suggest an annulment. So long as Marston continued to support her family financially, she'd been prepared to act as his wife and pretend the pub wasn't a convenient façade for his antiquities trade.

Inwardly, she cringed. Had Harlowe's unsolicited attention convinced Marston to try again?

Possibly. But that wasn't the whole of it. Her husband's dark mood had lifted a few days ago when the shipment of goods he'd expected finally arrived. Marston had become calm, more attentive. Friendly, even.

Worried he might suspect her contemplated betrayal, she'd worked to be ever more agreeable and above reproach. Perhaps, with new riches locked in the back room, he was relaxed enough to be amorous?

"I've a gift for you." Marston leaned close. The warmth of his breath swept over her face, his words spoken with a suggestive lilt and laced with demand.

She swallowed. "A gift?"

He handed her a thin box and her heart sank. "Open it. I want you to wear it."

Her lips pressed into a thin line.

"Your glances at the ladies here have not gone unnoticed." He nodded, misinterpreting her disapproval. "As my wife, you should have one for yourself."

So much for her surreptitious peeks at the jewelry recently sold to his female customers. Not that anyone would blame her for looking. Constructed from grave goods, the necklaces were modern interpretations of ancient styles, most consisting of re-strung beads and amulets plucked from mummy windings. All of them replete with symbolism. Ankhs. Falcons. Gods and goddesses. An Eye of Horus. Scarabs holding sun discs with their wings outstretched.

"They are remarkably beautiful."

He nodded. "Only the best for customers of The Monocled Raven. But I've been remiss as a husband. This new line of old jewelry is turning heads—and quite the profit—yet my wife remains unadorned when she ought to be wearing the most stunning piece of them all."

As an advertisement? Her husband's enterprise was not hers. She wanted no part. And yet her family's pub had become the brand name for his business venture. It was beyond vexing to witness The Monocled Raven's reputation tarred with the same brush as his quasi-legal business. Enough was enough. This had to stop.

But for now, she would play along. She needed evidence for Mr. Black, verifiable proof that Marston had left behind the gray margins of unethical dealings and crossed into sales of stolen goods. To that end, this was no time to cause a fuss.

Forcing a smile, she cracked open the case. When her jaw dropped, her amazement was genuine. She stared at a pectoral depicting Isis and Nephthys on either side of a scarab, arms outstretched. Constructed of gold and inlaid with lapis lazuli, carnelian, and colored glass, the level of exquisite details worked into the features of the goddesses was stunning. An ancient piece recovered from the depths of a tomb and brought back into the light. Setting aside the fact that it belonged in a museum, such a necklace was utterly and completely inappropriate wear for someone who spent most of their public life acting as brewer, baker and bar maid.

Marston reached out, lifting the necklace from its black velvet, then indicated she should turn around with the twirl of a finger. Secured about her neck, the pectoral would serve both as an advertisement *and* as a reminder to all present, Harlowe included, that he and he alone possessed this woman.

Over her plain bodice, heavy metal suspended by beads fell against her breastbone. He fastened the clasp.

She pressed fingertips to the artifact and murmured the expected reply. "Thank you."

"You're quite welcome." Words murmured into her ear. "I've neglected my bride's needs. To that end, I have procured a stimulant that should ensure our efforts end with the desired outcome. Every woman longs for a child."

They did not.

She cut off the sharp intake of her breath and bit her tongue. Object? Deflect? She could do neither without alienating her husband and delaying—or destroying—her plans for Oxford.

"That's right," he hummed. His fingers trailed down her spine and the heavy, possessive weight of his hand landed at the small of her back. "Wait for me tonight. Wear the necklace and nothing else."

CHAPTER TWO

"Before dawn," Graham Leyburn informed the head agent. "But no one knows where."

"Doesn't know?" Black frowned. "Or won't tell you?"

Side by side, they stood in the shadowed recess of a door across from The Monocled Raven, waiting for their target to exit the pub. Easier to think of him that way. Once he'd called the man friend, but it had all been an illusion. No sentiment remained on his part.

The hour grew late. Most patrons departed. The window above the pub—owner's quarters—brightened, then grew dark. Julia taking to her bed.

Downstairs, Harlowe and company displayed no inclination to leave. They sat before the pub's mullioned windows tossing back one pint after another, content to serve themselves after the official closing.

Yet his informant Lady Tramontin had insisted in a

hushed and horrified whisper the cult planned to meet tonight. She was convinced her son and his wife were involved and wanted Graham to put a stop to this obsessive Egyptian nonsense.

If she was right, wherever they planned to meet couldn't be all that far away.

"Either. Both. Does it matter?" He'd been unable to gather any additional clues. Patrons of The Monocled Raven —a drastically altered crowd from his days as a customer— refused to speak with him. Other acquaintances grew tight-lipped when the pub was mentioned.

Black narrowed his eyes. "There's an easy way to handle this. If you would speak to her yourself—"

"Tomorrow." Graham pinched the bridge of his nose. No sooner had he set foot in London and delivered his report, elaborating upon the bare bones messages he'd sent by telegram, than the agent had ordered him to approach Julia.

He'd refused. Dragging her into their world without first exhausting other options was an unacceptable approach. It wasn't safe.

They'd been at a stalemate ever since.

Black argued in favor of searching the pub's storeroom for the device.

Graham insisted the missing Egyptian technology would not be housed on site. That searching the property would tip their hand, escalating the situation. That it was better to follow suspected individuals to their nighttime gathering and confiscate the clockwork scarab and all associated gadgetry.

Grumbling about the Queen, the Duke of Avesbury and

strained international relations, Black had reluctantly granted him twenty-four hours.

What was at stake? A syntholink and its paired tether-sync inquisitor stolen from the Ptah Institute. Prototype devices of great importance, lifted from a laboratory in the dead of night and spirited away by a brilliant, if secretive, Bedouin scientist best described as disgruntled and disillusioned. That same night a collection of antiquities, including an occupied mummy case, disappeared from the Egyptian West Bank in Luxor.

Coincidence?

Perhaps. Save mere days later rumors of a powerful Bedouin by the name of Saleh who could bring the dead to life began to circulate. Most chalked the stories up to hallucinogens inhaled by way of hookah, until intel began to suggest the two thefts might well be related.

An internal review at the Ptah Institute was ongoing when he and Hassan—an Egyptian agent—were tasked with locating and questioning Saleh to rule out any possible connection to the thefts. An assignment that sent them on a month-long chase.

They'd followed a trail of bizarre deaths and stories of visions sent by Khepri, the scarab god. All rumors centered around cultlike activities involving a mummy case and a dark-skinned man dressed as an ancient Egyptian high priest. From Egypt to the Ottoman Empire, through Italy and France—they always arrived a few days behind the latest deadly "ceremony". Finally, they'd nabbed their man, the missing scientist, at Calais. Alas, the antiquities shipment the

Egyptian "high priest" had been shepherding was already aboard a boat somewhere on the English Channel en route to its final destination.

One which Saleh would not divulge. He'd clamped his lips together and refused to answer a single question.

The French authorities were less than cooperative, declining to take the suspect into their custody and challenging the rights of the two agents to restrict a man's freedom on foreign soil without concrete evidence of theft or wrongdoing. Arguments had ensued. Insults were hurled in three languages. Telegrams zipped along wires and sea cables in an attempt to cut through red tape. All while the stolen items continued their journey, unattended and untraced.

Frustrated, they'd agreed to separate. While his colleague remained behind trying to arrange extradition to Egypt, Graham took the next boat to Dover, hoping to pick up the trail of the mummy case.

Which had led him to London and to the doorstep of The Monocled Raven.

The past months had been hot, dusty and exhausting. Much as he wished for a few hours to himself, if only to shake the last of the desert sand from his socks, there'd been no time for respite. No time to pull the peace offering he'd carried for endless miles from his suitcase. No time to formulate a way to approach Julia unseen.

For that reason alone, he wanted this case finished, wrapped up and tied with a bow.

"Promises, promises," Black grumbled at his side.

"Marston won't have involved her," Graham insisted. Did he truly believe that or was he trying to convince himself because he'd once hoped to make Julia *his* wife?

As if he'd ever stood a chance at enticing her into matrimony. From the beginning of their affair, she'd made it perfectly clear to him that she intended to marry Professor Marston. Not once had she deviated from her chosen path, no matter how many nights she'd slept in Graham's bed, wrapped in his arms, the silk of her skin warm beneath his lips.

"So you insist." Black shrugged. "But neither is she unaware of his activities. Or Harlowe's."

"You spoke with her?" His voice rose with each word. Marston, for all his affable demeanor, possessed a ruthless streak.

"I did. Covertly. Foundations were laid."

He swallowed back a low growl. Black was his superior and had laughed off his concerns.

Black continued, "I approached Mrs. Marston with an offer to leave her position at the British Museum and work instead within the hallowed halls of the Lister Institute. She declined, angling for a position at Oxford instead."

"And you replied?"

"That I'd see it arranged. I expect she'll come around."

Graham did not.

Devoted to cataloging the archeological history of yeast in the production of bread and beer, Julia was unlikely to turn on a sixpence and instead devote her efforts to curing ringworm or thrush in human patients.

"When I returned the next morning," Black continued, "to inform her that a position in the History Department had been arranged, her reply was forestalled by the approach of footsteps. She all but shoved me out the kitchen door, loudly informing me the pub was not yet open."

"Professor Marston?"

Black shrugged. "Or an employee." He shot Graham a dagger-sharp look. "I've yet to receive her formal response in the affirmative."

Meaning he was to extract one. An academic position in exchange for information leading to the arrest of her husband and his assistant, Reed Harlowe.

"Fine," he grumbled, though he would not force her cooperation. "If tonight is unsuccessful, I'll find a way to speak with her tomorrow." He glanced again at his pocket watch and sighed. It was nearly three in the morning. "Today."

It wasn't that he didn't want to speak to Julia, only that he'd not wanted to approach her as an agent. He touched the carefully corked vial tucked inside his coat pocket. Special efforts had been required to obtain and return with the gift he carried over his heart. One he'd kept secret from Black as he refused to use it as a bribe.

Unfortunately, his gift languished for lack of proper care and ought to be delivered into her hands posthaste. And so he'd stalled for time, pondering how he might manage to separate professional from personal.

A few minutes later, finally, the last of the pub's patrons began to trickle out onto Fleet Street, laughing and shoulder thumping as they took leave of each other before scattering into the night.

The agents made no move until—

"Is that Reed Harlowe?" Black asked.

"It is."

Last to exit The Monocled Raven, Graham's old friend strolled down the street with a woman glued to his side, her steps unsteady. Intoxicated. The perfect excuse to wrap his arm about her waist, to pull her close. A seduction of dubious morality or a clever performance?

"Looks like a private meeting for two." Black snorted. "You're certain it's tonight, that he's involved?"

"Neck deep. He always is. And an expert at convincing you of his innocence."

"The professor is the one with the funds to make purchases."

Graham nodded. "True. Yet he grows complacent, leans too hard on those beneath him. Every acquaintance in London tasked with monitoring his actions reports that Harlowe covertly undermines Marston at every turn. The professor might be fronting the money, but there's no doubt in my mind who's running tonight's show."

"And if you're wrong?"

"I'll enlist the help of Mrs. Marston."

Black threw him a look. Waited.

Graham sighed. "Today."

They followed Harlowe and his paramour at a discreet distance as the couple wound their way through London's streets, heads tipped together, giggling. Overly innocent and saccharine behavior, even in their intoxicated state. But enough of an eye-rolling distraction that it wasn't until the pair circled back on themselves, retracing earlier steps, that Black came around to Graham's line of thinking.

The agent tossed him a dark glance. "Clever ruse to draw us away and waste our time?"

Graham nodded, his lips a flat line. A full hour had passed. "Intentional distraction. If we interfere, he'll claim to know nothing."

"We ought to have waited, followed Marston."

"Assuming he's involved in this particular deal." But Graham was beginning to doubt his instincts. "The professor has always preferred his illicit activity to come in shades of gray. Stolen government technology is a drastic departure from past norms and crosses a decided line into black, a color with which his protégé is comfortable."

Months of working at the British Museum alongside him had taught him Harlowe was not to be taken at face value. At first, they'd been friends of a sort, but on more than one occasion, he'd witnessed Harlowe sidle over to a classmate's library carrel and flip through unattended notes.

At Graham's objection, he'd shrugged. "Curiosity, nothing more."

And Graham might have left it at that, accepting his explanation, had—after one of those very students was dismissed for "academic misconduct"—Harlowe not submitted a monograph on an identical topic not one week later. Concerns he'd brought to Professor Marston, the man's mentor, only to watch them be brushed aside. Slowly, over time, small incidents, all easily dismissed on an individual basis, accumulated.

Which was why it was still possible that Julia, while aware of her husband's antiquities dealings on the black market and Harlowe's involvement, might not yet know of his plans to supplant the professor. In business. In academia. And, Graham suspected, in marriage.

None of which would come to pass if he could catch the scoundrel red-handed in possession of top-secret Egyptian technology. Preferably tonight.

At long last the drunken couple turned a corner onto a narrow lane, one where the buildings drew close and the streetlamps dared not follow. They stumbled up a set of stairs and—after Harlowe fumbled with a key—all but fell through the front door of a townhome.

"High odds their romantic proclivities serve as a decoy?" Black asked. "That he'll abandon the woman to climb out a back window, hop over a fence and be on his way?"

"Precisely what I would expect of —" The fine hairs on the back of Graham's neck registered a shadow.

He spun on his heel, searching the contours of the moonlit gloom behind them. An outline shifted and a black, clockwork dog with tall, pointed ears stepped forward. Gold edged its every feature, tracing outlines of its eyes, ears, nose and mouth. A golden collar emblazoned with an ankh encircled its neck. Around the ankles of its forelegs glinted gold bracelets.

"Anubis." The name emerged on breath of disbelief as he reached out to tap Black's shoulder. Well-oiled and painstakingly calibrated, Anubis—god of death and the underworld, guardian of tombs—made not a single sound as it stepped forward on metallic paws. Uncanny and decidedly ominous, but not outright threatening. "We've a potential problem."

Before the last word had left Graham's lips, Black was pounding on the door.

It flew open and a bleary-eyed, old woman in a nightcap glowered at them.

"A word with Mr. Harlowe."

"Harlowe!" The woman bellowed. "Neighbors are complaining about that bloody dog again!"

"Where?" Graham demanded, pushing past the woman and into the hall.

She sighed. "Top of the stairs, door on the left."

They ran up the stairs and, before Graham could raise his fist, the door opened.

"You're interrupting." Harlowe grinned at him, cravat loose about his neck. Slender bare arms were wrapped about his torso, fingertips working to set waistcoat buttons free. The man caught at them, stopping their progress. Giggles erupted behind him. "Are you here to beg for help? I can probably get Marston to let you work at the museum again. For a price."

"Unnecessary." Graham narrowed his eyes, shifted his coat to the side providing a glimpse of his holstered TTX weapon. "I've been cleared."

"Oh, have you now?" Harlowe sneered. "Always the moral one. Until Julia. But we all have our weaknesses."

"Speaking of price tags." Black stepped forward. "That

clockwork Anubis of yours, did you purchase it directly from its Bedouin maker?"

"Jackal, actually." Harlowe clucked his tongue and shook his head. "But he's not mine. Marston recently acquired him, but I'll warn you that he's already turned down more than one gypsy's offer to purchase his guardian."

Black stiffened.

"You misunderstand," Graham stated. "You are suspected of receiving stolen Egyptian goods."

"Is this about the mummy?" the woman asked, drawing his attention to the amulet that hung about her neck.

Graham lifted his eyebrows. An Eye of Horus. Protection from evil. Mere decoration, or was she—like many others before her—convinced of its power?

Harlowe drew back, pried the woman's hands from his waist, spinning her about. "Hush, Mina. Sit. Over there." She pouted but crossed the small room to slouch upon an unmade bed. Her would-be-lover turned back to them. "I act as Marston's assistant. Nothing we sell is stolen. If it's paperwork you want, it can wait until business hours."

"I'm certain everything will *appear* in order." Black leaned to look past Harlowe. "Illegally possessed items are rarely kept where anyone might view them."

Harlowe threw open the door. "Search away."

With no compunction, they did exactly that. A number of items— a bronze torc, a bronze penannular brooch with a rusty pin, a silver bowl with beaten silver panels of figures wrestling animals—ought not have been in his apartments, but as they openly rested atop a desk alongside artifacts

Graham knew supported the man's Celtic research project, he said nothing. Not so much as a whisper about the man finally sticking to a course of study. A case could be made that these objects were on temporary loan for study purposes. Neither, however, did he nor Black find anything of interest tucked away in drawers or hidden among his other possessions.

He and the agent shared a frustrated glance. They'd been led astray, purposefully distracted.

"Where is Marston?" Graham demanded. He'd picked the wrong target. Time to correct his mistake.

"Home in bed with his lovely young wife?" The words were spoken as a taunt. The love triangle a poorly hidden if unspoken secret.

"I very much doubt that." Graham crossed his arms. "Not if there's profit involved."

"Coinciding with a macabre trend to fashion jewelry from grave goods." Black lifted an eyebrow.

Harlowe heaved an exasperated sigh, tossed a regretful glance at Mina. "Marston told me that he'd handle the mummy unwrapping himself."

Graham frowned. Amusement in the form of archeological desecration, an irretrievable loss of academic knowledge in pursuit of profit. Such unwrapping parties rarely bothered to document the process by which the entertainer unwound the ancient, yellowed linen from the body of a man or woman who'd lived in the Twenty-First Dynasty some two thousand years ago.

Marston knew better. Yet, it seemed, no longer bothered to practice what he preached.

They stared at Harlowe, letting silence stretch until the man filled the void.

"This was to be my night off," he groused. "Mummy unwrapping parties were all the rage a generation ago. At this point, they're old hat. We know what's tucked inside all the dry, dusty linen. But there's always someone who insists on holding an event, who wants to see for themselves. And Marston aims to please. For a price, he'll throw a private party complete with Egyptian-themed costumes and backdrops."

"Inside a theater?" Covent Garden was but a few streets away. Were any of the plays set in sandy, foreign lands? Graham had been away from the city too long to know what performances might be current.

Black grimaced, perhaps recalling the nearby blazing catastrophe from which he'd pulled two of his agents.

Harlowe lifted a shoulder. "He mentioned something about a tomb. If so, I'm surprised he did not take the jackal with him. For protection. But operating such a creature is illegal inside city limits." A wicked glint sparked in his eyes, his next words no better than a sharp stick jabbed in his side. "You could try Nicholas Hawksmoor's Pyramid at St. Anne's Church, Limehouse."

Graham narrowed his eyes but said nothing. A deliberate misdirection. No self-respecting Egyptologist would ever consider the Freemason tomb remotely authentic. And yet the man's comment was a pointed hint at where they might find the professor. Not that he trusted Harlowe to give him the correct location. Always manipulating the situation to his advantage, no matter who might be hurt in the process.

They asked a few more questions, received even fewer answers in return. None of them were helpful.

Graham tipped his head, letting Black know they ought to leave.

As they exited the boarding house, Anubis, unblinking and still, sat beside the doorstep. Death and tombs were repeating themes this evening.

"You know where to find Marston." Black's comment was a statement, not a question.

London, with its dangerously overcrowded parish burial grounds leaking decaying matter into the water supply, had established several large suburban cemeteries. A number of them were notable for their architectural elements. In particular, the architect of one cemetery an hour due north had succumbed to Egyptomania and placed an entire structure—the Egyptian Avenue and Circle of Lebanon—at its very heart.

Graham nodded. "Highgate Cemetery."

CHAPTER THREE

Utterly ridiculous, her behavior.

She was a scientist. She ought not be glancing over her shoulder unable to shake the feeling, the vague sensation, the creeping suspicion that someone—or some*thing*—watched. Then again, she was tramping through Highgate Cemetery at the crack of dawn. Were she truly immune to the tales of hauntings and stories of ghostly wraiths, spirits and souls reported to wander the grounds in the hours between dusk and dawn, she might have visited last evening when Harlowe dropped the bug in her ear about a fairy ring beneath a pine tree.

Chasing after the mushroom caps that formed fairy rings felt like a decided shift in her research focus. But there were traditional drinks, both beer and wine, made from fermented mushrooms. She wasn't abandoning archeological mycology, she was expanding the scope of her historical research. A nod to the fae merely added a touch of whimsy to the project.

Would Marston allow her to accept an academic appointment at Oxford? He might frown upon his wife working for an institution that occasionally came into conflict with his own. Would he insist she remain in London if only to help run the pub? Or, alternatively, would he wave an inconvenient wife swiftly on her way so that he might expand his business without her oversight and disapproval?

Questions that weighed upon her chest at night like the lid of a stone sarcophagus.

Something rustled in the nearby froth of ferns, brakes and gorse—the sprawling undergrowth that surrounded the monoliths, mausoleums and burial vaults—and she skittered sideways. But only a single step. A fox, perhaps, wrapping up its nighttime patrol. Or a squirrel. Certainly nothing supernatural. Absolutely not.

Dead was dead and there were no such things as fairies, elves or pixies. Ridiculous to even imagine such beings would deign to inhabit space within London, let alone suggest that some prehistoric and malicious entity skulked beneath the broad spread of tree limbs in Highgate.

Still, she quickened her steps, scanning the ground beneath every coniferous tree for *Tricholoma*.

A few minutes to study the fairy circle. A handful more to collect a few specimens, and she'd be on her way back to the bright, noisy streets of London where the only wraiths that would worry her were the dexterous children that moved through crowds silently and efficiently plucking valuables from pockets.

There. She all but bounced on her toes.

Mushrooms grew beneath a pine on the verge of the pathway, with the ring formation encroaching upon a single gravesite—the setting haunting and poignant. *Tricholoma* was a tricky genus when it came to foraging. Species could be edible, inedible or outright poisonous—and accurate identification could be difficult. Matsutake mushrooms, a variety rare on the British Isles, would be the perfect specimens for fermenting into a fruity, spicy ale.

Fingers crossed that these were edible, she drew closer.

All signs were favorable—the fungi possessed light brown caps, classic in form and size, but she would need to tease away the soil to confirm the presence of thick white stems. She bent at the waist, tipping the mushroom cap upward to confirm white-spored gills beneath. But found yellow ones instead—a faint glowing yellow.

Bioluminescence. He'd been telling the truth after all.

She blinked.

Biological light was almost always blue, but green could be found in *Panellus stipticus*, the bitter oyster mushroom that grew on logs and glowed gently in the woods. But these particular specimens were decidedly yellow, perhaps even a light amber. The tree canopy above scattered the light, dimming it such that the fruiting bodies of the fairy ring might resemble small lamps set in a circle, the better to illuminate the tiny feet of dancing pixies.

She brightened. Visions of monographs danced in her head. Not a wasted trip after all.

She'd had doubts, wondered if Harlowe had sent her on a wild-goose chase. That there would be no fairy ring, no pine-mushrooms at all. More than once on the trip here—by tube, omnibus and crank hack—she'd wondered if his "revelation" was a teasing lie formulated to chase her from the pub such that he and her husband might conduct a shady antiquities sale at dawn without worrying about the inconvenience of a wife nearby in the kitchen baking bread.

After all, her husband had failed to appear in her bedroom last night.

Julia set down her basket and pulled out measuring tape, notebook and pencil from her hip pouch. Careful not to step into the center—some habits, superstition or otherwise, were hard to break—she recorded a diameter of some forty-two inches. A small ring. The caps ranged in sizes from an inch and a half to about three—

A movement at the edge of her visual field turned her head. *What was that?*

Nothing but an immobile stone angel crouched atop a headstone staring at her through a thick green tangle of ivy.

Nerves. It was only her nerves. Working alone in a necropolis would tug on the loose threads of anyone's instincts.

She took a deep breath, shoved her notes back into the basket and pulled out a small trowel. Destroying the fairy ring would be nothing short of a crime. But removing two or three mushrooms wouldn't significantly impact the circle's growth.

Stooping over, she dug into the soil beneath the mushroom, careful to collect a portion of the underground mycorrhizal network as she freed the thick-stemmed fruiting body from the ground. She smiled. Matsutake, she was all but certain.

Before she could set about brewing a matsutake ale, she would need a much larger supply and that meant propagation. Given the species formed a symbiotic relationship via the roots of a pine tree, there would be inherent difficulties with the process of encouraging the mycelium to spread through substrate under laboratory conditions.

Trial and error she was willing to throw herself into no matter the weeks, months and possibly years it might require to optimize growth, to pin down the mushroom's preferred ecological co-species. Until then, however, she needed a pine sapling to ensure the health of the matsutake mushrooms. She'd watch over them carefully. First a terrarium, later a dedicated portion of the rooftop garden. There were toxicology profiles to run and the unusual bioluminescence to consider. Excitement zinged through her body. She might even need to designate one of the fruiting bodies as a holotype specimen and name a new species.

From her basket, she pulled a sheet of waxed paper. Onto this went the entirety of her sample. Rolling the paper to form a tube, she folded the ends, tying a bit of twine about the tips to secure the contents. She tucked the packet inside the basket, then set about retrieving a second specimen and two small pine saplings just in case one failed to thrive.

The stand of ferns to her left quivered and a cluster of tiny mushrooms poked its head out from between the fronds.

She froze, mouth open. *What in the red-capped mushroom rabbit hole?*

Fungi ought not have pointy legs. They were sessile. Immobile. Some might say rooted, though she would argue otherwise. Hyphae might resemble roots, but they were part of the larger mycelium, yet certainly did not render a mushroom ambulatory. Rather the opposite. Moreover, no such creature as a mushroom in possession of limbs existed. A least, not to her knowledge. And that was before she addressed the presence of a head with compound eyes.

For a long moment, they stared at each other, then the creature shifted and dappled sunlight glinted off a copper and blue carapace. Ah, a fungal-infested insect. That made much more sense. Poor thing. She'd read a monograph once about insects with their will subverted and redirected to the bidding of colonizing parasitic fungi so as to reach locations optimal for spore dispersal, but—

Wait.

She squinted at the palm-sized beetle. Were those gears hidden just beneath its wing casings? Hard to tell with all the fruiting bodies sprouting from its thorax. A clockwork creature? She tipped her head, angling for a clearer view. A balance wheel propelled by a spiral torsion spring emitted a low mechanical whir as it spun. Clockwork? What was more alive, the insect or the tiny mushrooms? She voted the latter. But why would such fungus be growing on a copper clockwork contraption when there was no organism to control and no organic material to consume?

Very carefully and very slowly, she crept forward, intending to cage the clockwork fungus creature, when the whir rose to an irritating buzz and the clockwork creature dashed into the undergrowth, carrying its fungal passengers along for the ride.

She chased after the insect, shoving aside spindly branches and hanging vines searching for the glint of sunlight on copper. Light flashed. There, darting beneath a hawthorn bush. With a lunge that landed a foot on the hem of her skirts and all but sent her sprawling, she upended her basket and slammed it down over the scurrying champignon beetle, falling hard upon her hip as she twisted to avoid crashing into a memorial headstone.

"Ha!" Not one, but two discoveries in one morning. Triumphant, she shoved onto her hands and knees, careful to keep a palm pressed down atop the basket as she shifted to fight the tangle she'd made of her skirts.

Which was when she found herself face to face with a half-naked body that lay prostrate upon the ground, head turned to the side, eyes open and unseeing. Recognition flashed. An electric jolt of lightning zinged along her nerves and set her heart pounding and crashing against her ribcage. She shoved at plants and leaf litter, her fingers digging into the soil, abandoning her basket to frantically crawl backward away from an all too familiar visage indelibly imprinted upon her retinas.

The wiry gray hairs at his temples, the hawkish nose threaded with burst capillaries, the waxed and twisted ends of a mustache he'd fussed with endlessly as the terms of their marriage contract were negotiated. A binding legal contract that permitted him to sink his claws into the family business, one her father refused to allow his eldest child, a woman, to manage on her own. Terms to which she'd agreed—after careful review of the documents and several revisions to spell out with extreme specificity the particulars of her inheritance and freedoms as his spouse. Keen to take a sweet young thing as his wife, a common enough practice when a man required heirs or preferred morality to a mistress, he'd agreed to a number of her demands.

Her husband was neither old nor young but hovered somewhere in-between. She'd expected to endure a decade or two as his spouse. Certainly not less than a year. Hence her attentiveness to every detail.

Now Angus Marston was dead. Her hated husband, dead.

Free! No longer chained to his bad decisions she could—

No.

No rejoicing.

His death might instead be a curse. Would his clients hurl unfounded accusations and spread vicious rumors, anything to avoid scrutiny?

Only last night they'd conversed. He'd announced his intentions yet failed to appear. Only to be found dead on the forest floor of Highgate Cemetery? Wearing nothing but sandals, a linen skirt and a striped head covering? She frowned. There were golden armbands wrapped about his wrists. And a necklace—a heavy pectoral—hung around his neck.

She blinked. Why was he dressed in imitation of an Egyptian pharaoh?

Harlowe would know. A notion that stabbed ice into her heart and sent suspicion ripping outward.

So much for his benevolent direction of her attention to a pine-mushroom fairy ring. Would he have bothered to inform her of its existence if he'd not wanted Mrs. Marston precisely where she was? In guilty proximity to her dead husband, unable to account for his behavior?

She pressed a hand to her chest, willing herself to draw in deep, steadying breaths. Panic would gain her nothing.

As her mind turned over one implication after the other, the fungus-encrusted mechanical insect tipped up the edge of her forgotten basket. She stretched an arm out to slap the wicker cage back in place, to secure the strange biomechanical device. But she was a moment too late. The infested beetle scurried out into the light, stretched its wings wide and took flight.

Which was when she finally recognized the species upon which the contraption had been modeled. The escapee was an oversized, copper clockwork scarab.

Her gaze fell upon her husband. Egyptian scarab. Egyptian costume. And—not far from here—the Egyptian Avenue and its tombs.

Midnight mushrooms!

Her hands fisted in her skirts. She could flee, pretend surprise when the authorities inevitably arrived at her doorstep. But that would mean discarding the pine-mushroom project. Impossible to publish without making note of their provenance as the location of their discovery was key.

No. There was no escaping their questions. She was innocent of all wrongdoing and refused to abandon such a spectacular discovery on the outskirts of London. Fortifying herself with a deep breath, she braced herself to continue her work. It would be the matter of minutes to collect two more pine-mushrooms, wrap them in paper and tuck them inside her basket.

She glanced about, looking for her trowel.

Only then did she notice where she sat.

Dead center in the middle of the fairy ring.

A forlorn cry escaped her lips. Not because she worried the pixies would retaliate or that time would be altered when she stepped from the circle, but because her mad scramble had torn free a number of the mushroom caps, forever altering the natural outward progression of the underground mycelium.

"Julia?"

Her heart stopped. The air in her lungs froze, all moisture within instantly crystalized into sharp spikes of icy pain.

"Graham?" The name emerged on a puff of her breath, a ghost of a whisper.

To be discovered in a graveyard beside one's dead spouse by one's former lover? Bad. Even worse? He was accompanied by Mr. Black, a man who had—only days past—attempted to recruit her with an Oxford offer in exchange for providing evidence of Marston's involvement in illegal antiquities trafficking.

Perhaps the elves were about to toy with her life after all.

CHAPTER FOUR

Graham placed no credence in the existence of the little people or the various mischievous games they purportedly played with humans. Nor did he believe in curses. Humans were quite capable of causing innumerable problems for themselves and others without any kind of supernatural intervention by imaginary species.

And in this case, there were an abundance of suspects who were all too human.

Including Graham himself.

Professor Marston had assigned him the role of scapegoat, complicating his life to the point Graham had needed to abandon England's shores. Which made it that much more disappointing to find his accuser dead upon the ground, his eyes open and turned to the sky, his face a mask of shock and terror. Graham had looked forward to metaphorically holding the man's feet to the fire and forcing a detailed confession. But someone—or something—had gotten to him first.

Adding a certain difficulty to the investigation.

He found himself grateful Black made for a solid alibi.

Holding up a hand, indicating Black and Julia should be silent and still, he took several steps backward, scanning for any hints of movement that might indicate someone watched from behind nearby trees or gravestones.

There. A few feet away, the branches of a bush were bent. Leaves ripped away in a manner that suggested Marston had stumbled through the undergrowth without much forethought or care. Had he been running from something? Someone?

Given how the man had treated everyone as his inferior, it would not surprise Graham if he found a wild-eyed murderer lurking in the undergrowth, fingers wrapped around a blunt object.

Carefully, he circled the scene.

Last fall, when the professor learned of his fiancée's affair, he'd seethed and fumed.

With reason.

Graham and Julia were in the wrong. She'd made promises, ones that both of them had ignored over the course of several weeks.

But Marston had also made threats to Graham's career, ones he'd acted upon. And those had gone a step too far.

Part of a shipment to the British Museum for a special exhibit—ancient Egyptian faience amulets—went missing. A search was launched, but to no avail. The crate of artifacts had vanished as if swallowed by the night. Marston leveled an unsubstantiated accusation at the visiting Rankine engineering student and stood by, smug, as eyebrows and questions were raised.

Had Graham taken advantage, leveraged lack of oversight and unfettered access to all things faience that he might feather his pockets at the expense of the archeological museum?

He snorted. The irony. By then the professor and his minion were already proficient at supplementing their incomes on the black market and in need of a legitimate business to conceal their activity.

Graham glanced behind a few inordinately large gravestones, but found nothing. He moved on.

To this day he remained certain the professor and Harlowe had quickly transferred the stolen items into the hands of greedy collectors, removing all evidence before implicating the one man who threatened Marston's matrimonial plans.

In the end, nothing could be proven.

But the damage was done.

With his career crumbling, Graham had been at a loss. Not a single ranking individual at the museum dared speak out against the prominent Egyptologist to defend a lowly student, particularly one not of their institution.

Which was when a Mr. Black stepped into the fray, smoothed ruffled feathers and chased away the carrion eaters before offering Graham a way to clear his name: step away from London and work as an undercover Queen's agent while employed as an archaeological engineer in Egypt. There he could use his XRF analyzer to study faience amulets in the field. Should the Crown require his services, he would act as an agent to assist British interests abroad.

Graham had readily agreed. He'd informed Julia with terse words that he would be leaving for the archaeological season and, upon his return, would move his studies back to the Rankine Institute. That they need not ever cross paths again. He'd waited for her to object, to beg him to stay. But though pain crossed her face, a not unexpected, and perhaps inevitable, silence had stretched between them until he turned upon his heel and walked away.

Such was the last time they'd been in each other's company.

Finding no evidence the professor had been followed, he rejoined the others beside the dead man.

"Any signs of physical violence?" he asked.

"Nothing overt," Black answered. "But an autopsy is certainly warranted."

Both of them turned speculative gazes upon Julia. A wife was always a suspect, especially an unhappy one. She'd married for money, for security. Her husband had been old enough to be her father and, though such spring-fall weddings were far from rare, rumors would inevitably circulate.

Ought he have tried harder to convince her not to sacrifice her happiness for that of her family?

Perhaps.

Over and again he'd told himself the abrupt end to their

relationship was for the best. Permanent physical distance between them would keep his presence from reminding Marston of the past, prompting yet more retaliation.

Moreover, it would spare himself the heartache of her rejection.

Or so he'd believed.

For a few months, he'd thrown himself into a new project in a new country and experienced—relative—peace.

Then classified Egyptian technology had been stolen from the Ptah Institute on the same day as the Egyptian Museum's theft. Soon, a telegram arrived from Black. Graham's orders: assist the Egyptians in recovering their property.

Such had been the beginning of his odyssey home.

Upon discovering the trail of breadcrumbs led to none other than the eminently respectable Professor Marston and his minion, Graham had happily set his teeth for revenge. Until he'd realized there would likely be collateral damage: the man's wife.

That the woman happened to be Julia, Graham's former lover?

Well, that complicated the situation.

He'd hoped to keep her out of this investigation, for his own peace of mind as much as to preserve her reputation. Alas, she was now in the thick of things. Could he set aside his personal feelings?

"Graham? Why are you—" White knuckled, her hands clutching fistfuls of weeds and twigs, Julia's gaze slid over to the half-naked body, but quickly leapt away.

Yes. Marston's state of undress beside a pool of vomit was indeed disturbing. What she didn't know was that his clumsy attempt at recreating ancient Egyptian dress was also damning.

"Here? You know why." He kept this voice soft, considerate. Whatever her feelings for her husband, there would be social and economic consequences. "Mr. Black informed me he spoke with you about your husband's illicit activities." And had identified himself as an agent of the Crown.

Julia nodded. "He did. You work with him?"

"I do." *With. For.* These past few days it had alternated according to circumstances.

"How can this possibly involve the Rankine Institute?" The was a slight hesitation in her voice and confusion tightened her face. "Or your engineering work in material analysis?" Her narrow-eyed considering gaze shifted to Black. "Suspicions of black-market smuggling are entirely different from—" She waved a hand at the body. "This. I have no explanation for his state of dress. Or his presence here. Nor for his... demise."

He quirked an eyebrow. That last bit was a lie. Or part of one. He wasn't quite certain yet, but she knew something.

Black lifted a shoulder but said nothing.

"Does it?" She turned back toward Graham with wide blue eyes.

Innocence? Dismay? Or was that guilt swimming about, floundering, unable to latch on to a logical explanation as to how she came to be planted in the midst of a ring of faintly glowing mushrooms on a swath of leaf litter and pine-needles in a graveyard beside her dead husband?

It was a lot to take in. For him. For her. And this was before he informed her of her husband's probable involvement in an Egyptian-themed cult. But the man was dead now. Such was the silver lining of a lead coffin. Was there anything left between them worth salvaging?

Perhaps time spent together might turn into the beginning of something new, rather than the end of something old.

They could start by working the case together and see where that led. A relief, in some ways, to stop hiding, to reveal the entirety of his new life such that he might keep her safe by his side.

Graham held out a hand, pulling her onto her feet and away from the crushed and broken fairy circle. Her soft palm placed in his reawakened sleeping nerve endings. They snapped awake in a sudden rush of awareness and hummed in anticipation, heedless of their presence in a graveyard. All they remembered was the soft satin of her skin as they gripped eager hips while she arched over him and—

Suddenly his collar was too tight, his wool coat an overly thick weave for a summer morning, and his trousers tailored a touch too small for easy movement.

They'd agreed to terms beforehand. A brief affair. A few nights of physical indulgence before she spoke her vows.

Logic had dictated her decision. A husband like Marston had had much to offer her—far beyond anything Graham might have hoped to provide. Protection, position, opportunities. Not that it stopped his heart from cracking and bleeding every time she'd slipped from between his sheets and crept away under cover of darkness.

He was dragged back to the current crisis when Black muttered something unintelligible under his breath about his two best suspects investigating the case.

"No explanation?" the head agent prompted. "No idea what business your husband had in Highgate Cemetery late last night, Mrs. Marston?"

"None," she said. "We do not—did not—consult each other concerning our individual activities."

"Yet here you are," Black replied. "Beside him. I'm not in the habit of dismissing coincidences."

"Nor am I." She frowned. "I assure you I had no knowledge of my husband's nighttime whereabouts. We occupy separate sleeping quarters."

A statement that pricked Graham's ears. He filed that piece of information away for later.

She continued. "I last saw him in the company of friends in the taproom shortly before I retired upstairs at midnight. I arrived at the cemetery less than an hour ago with no expectation of meeting anyone." A shaking hand gestured at an overturned basket, at a collection of twine and waxed paper that fluttered in the light breeze. "Last evening I was informed of the presence of a glowing fairy ring. That the mushrooms were little lamps illuminating tiny feet as they spun and danced. I came to investigate, to collect a specimen."

Of course the pub was involved. When did The Monocled Raven not figure into her calculations? But fairy *magic*?

Had he badly misjudged her commitment to the methodology of scientific inquiry?

Black's eyebrows rose. "Not two days ago, you informed me your work centered about the advent of agriculture, the production of beer and its influence upon leavened bread. Now you study fairies?"

Unease rippled across her face, but she squared her shoulders. "Not fairies. Nor other mythological creatures such as elves or pixies. I'm a historical mycologist. I study fungus, which includes, but is not limited to, the singular cellular yeasts that form bubbles in beer and bread. Fungi also encompasses mushrooms. Such as the Scotch bonnet, the fruiting bodies of which grow in a ring formation and have inspired any number of myths and fairy tales. This particular pine-mushroom is edible. Moreover, as is relevant to my research, it is traditionally fermented into a number of alcoholic beverages. I would never—" She skewered Black with a sharply-honed stare. "—propose that supernatural creatures with an affinity for the genus *Tricholoma* might be responsible for tempting a man into a circular enclosure to dance to his death."

"Yet, there lies your husband," Black countered with a brusque nod of his head. "Barefoot and bare-chested. And quite undeniably dead."

"And here you are, two agents of the Crown, tasked with investigating all things aimed at mixing biology with technology to a nefarious end." She'd done the calculus and reached the correct conclusion. "I think we can rule out the fae."

"True." Black gave Graham a meaningful look, then made a circular gesture with his hand, indicating that it was his case and he ought to take the lead.

An uncomfortable silence fell among them, never mind the chirping of birds, the rustle of leaves and the faint and distant sounds of city traffic.

"Who?" Graham found his voice. "Who mentioned the fairy circle?"

Color rose high upon her cheeks. "Harlowe."

A red haze clouded his vision. Harlowe had begun his studies in the Egyptology Department about the same time Graham had received permission to analyze ceramic Egyptian statues using nondestructive cathode ray spectroscopy. A few weeks later, Julia had arrived seeking access to an ancient Egyptian papyrus detailing the medicinal use of beer.

Though they'd both eyed her intoxicating curves and basked in the brilliance of her mind, friendship made them agree: no courting. Not that either of them had—at the time—the means to support a wife. Instead, they would treat her as a sister.

Yet not a month later, Harlowe had openly attempted to entice her to his boarding house. Julia turned him down firmly, laughing at the absurdity. As if his words were in jest. But Graham had caught the wicked glint in his eyes and resolved to keep an eye out for any further underhanded advances.

Over time, the three friends drifted apart. A natural academic progression as the work of each scholar grew specialized, each spending more and more time upon the minutiae particular to their chosen thesis.

Harlowe had run into difficulties with his proposed thesis in Egyptology and turned to drink to smooth the rough edges, nearly giving up entirely when they proved too sharp. For a while, he'd fallen in with those who sought to revive the practices of the druids. Which, given those long-ago Celts had committed nothing to paper, more or less involved inventing an entire religion anew.

Graham's work, however, proceeded apace. Locked away in the basement of the museum pointing his electronic contraption at one artifact after the next, he'd almost missed Julia's growing distress. Her academic work had suffered under the pressures her family imposed upon her.

One evening, he'd made a point of stopping by The Monocled Raven—and found Harlowe ensconced in a booth, already deep in his cups. Harried, Julia joined them for a moment, long enough to impart the distressing news of her engagement to Professor Marston.

Harlowe had objected. As had Graham. But she was resolute. They'd argued, but the pub was in financial distress and there was no changing her mind. She intended to save her sisters' futures at the cost of her own.

Both Graham and Harlowe had attempted to drink away their misery. With his head start, Harlowe soon slumped in his chair, asleep. Which was when Julia returned to proposition Graham.

Had Harlowe heard her murmured words? Or Graham's whispered acceptance?

He couldn't prove it was Harlowe who told the professor that his fiancée was involved in an illicit *affaire de coeur* beneath his very nose. Nor did he know for certain that Harlowe was the architect of his fall. But it was fully in character for Harlowe to suggest killing two birds with one stone: sell a few antiquities on the black market for fun and profit, then blame Julia's lover, the outsider, to cover their trail.

All while eyeing his mentor's wife and pondering how she might be stolen away.

With his romantic rival banished from the country, Harlowe enjoyed a rapid rise to archaeological prominence in his new field, aided by his status as Marston's second-in-command for all extracurricular antiquity transactions. A position that no doubt reflected positively on his bank statement. But it also complicated any relationship he might try to strike up with Julia. So long as she was legally bound to Marston, Harlowe wouldn't have risked chasing after her skirts.

But that was then and this was now.

Everything had changed. As of this morning, Julia was a widow. Had Harlowe helped to engineer such a state in order to claim her hand? Or was it simply a happy byproduct of an attempt to take over her husband's business?

Graham suffered a brief pang that, upon learning of the man's death, his own first thought had been of the opportunity it presented. But theirs was a romance with a past shaped by mutual attraction rather than by familial arm-twisting and failing finances.

"Harlowe?" he repeated. By now, steam must be pouring

from his ears. "Why would you trust a single damn thing that falls from his lips? He only ever acts in his own interests." Had he set her up as the dupe, deliberately sent her to Highgate Cemetery? He rather thought so. And given the expression on her face, she agreed.

"Glowing. Fairy. Ring." She pronounced each word as if he were hard of hearing, a careful restatement of her earlier words underscored with a wave at her toppled basket. "Bioluminescent matsutake are undocumented. Add to that they are a fermentable fungi." Her backbone stiffened. "One does not simply accept a position at Oxford without a new and interesting research topic already in hand." She directed her last comment at Black, then took a deep breath. "Harlowe presented me with such irresistible lure at approximately a quarter till midnight. Possibly he hoped I'd venture here in the dark? Tempting. Nonetheless, I waited until dawn."

"Whereupon you stumbled over Marston's dead body," Graham pointed out. "Ultimately accomplishing his aim."

Black cleared his throat. "Both of you each possess a number of reasons to be pleased with Professor Marston's death. Both of you also have a problematic history with each other *and* the other remaining suspect." A spark of mischief flickered in his dark eyes. "Which means you will be investigating his death. Together." He lifted a hand as Julia sucked in her breath to voice a protest. "I'm no longer asking, Mrs. Marston. Clear your name. Then we will discuss if any academic appointments remain on the table."

"She's had quite the shock," Graham objected. "Take her

with me? We've already searched the grounds, which leaves—"

"The Egyptian-themed above-ground burial chambers. Yes." Black tossed Graham a black iron key. "That will allow you access. Think of it as keeping a handy suspect in close custody."

"I'm perfectly innocent," Julia huffed.

"Yet have knowledge of Marston's behavior and other activities," Black replied. "Therefore you have insight. Stolen technology and people are missing. Find them and we might have answers. It's not as if we can allow you to return home, not when your pub's storeroom may be filled with contraband."

The agent's points were good ones. And yet. "Involving her at this point also means she'll need to know about the scarab and the—"

"I'm aware." Black bent over the body and removed the pectoral Marston wore. He handed it to Graham. "Keep the ancient artifact safe. It doesn't belong in a morgue. Not only is it evidence, the museum will want it back."

He slid the heavy piece of jewelry into the inner pocket of his coat. "Will do."

"Bring Mrs. Marston up to speed while you search for the inquisitor along the Egyptian Avenue and the Circle of Lebanon. I'll head back to the steam carriage and send a skeet pigeon to call in Jackson and Pagett to render assistance and transport the body to Lister."

CHAPTER FIVE

er? A suspect in her husband's death?

Julia didn't care for the way her stomach twisted into knots. This agent of the Crown believed that she—or Graham or both!—could be accused? Of murder? Her eyes slid to her dead husband's body, then leapt away. Marston didn't look much like a murder victim. Rather a victim of misadventure. Then again, she'd no experience with dead bodies. Leastways, none of the recently alive variety. Mummies, she supposed, didn't count.

Her heart began to leap about inside her chest as if escape was possible. She wasn't guilty! Wishing someone dead was not a crime.

True, she found it hard to feign any kind of regret about Marston's sudden, unexpected passing. There were many times she'd hoped he'd reap the consequences of his activities sooner than later. She'd always assumed he'd be found in a back alley with a knife stuck in his back. Under no circumstances, however, had she imagined being the person to discover his remains.

Murdered and tossed into the bushes to await discovery by his unwitting, unfortunate wife sent there by none other her husband's right-hand man—

"Wait." The word emerged on a choke. "Did you say 'scarab'?" The very creature she'd watch run through the undergrowth away from her husband's body to take wing?

Graham nodded, looking pained. "I did."

Mushrooms on a log!

Her mind was processing this pretzel of a situation far too slowly, tripping and stumbling as she struggled to fit each piece in place. Events of recent months, particularly the last few weeks, flashed through her mind. Little incidents, seemingly inconsequential at the time, but taken as a whole?

Damning.

Anger welled up, accompanied by a cold sort of irritable resentment that sent a chill running through her veins, one that steadied her pulse. So much for her attempts to distance herself from the unabashed smuggling taking place in her pub.

Yes. *Hers.* Even more so as of this very moment. To run as she saw fit. No more need to leave London. But only if she could clear her name.

Which meant catching Harlowe red-handed, proving that he had orchestrated events that ended in this deadly mess. That she was no more than an innocent bystander, no matter her presence in the cemetery. At least she'd been assured of Graham's help. Even better, offered an active role in resolving this mess.

Though Graham hadn't offered. Rather, he'd been ordered.

His reappearance in her life, however traumatic, prompted the return of a dull heartache, of a longing she'd done her best to stuff into a dark corner and ignore. A misery that was her fault entirely. She regretted not listening to her heart's entreaties, ones that begged her to abandon her responsibilities, to run away with the man she loved. Instead, she'd allowed cold calculations to dictate her choice of a marriage partner.

And regretted it ever since.

Three old friends. One had played her false. No surprise there. A cold fire smoldered through her veins as she thought of all the times Harlowe had approached her, holding out a semblance of an olive branch in the form of fascinating tidbits that might be both interesting and relevant to her research. A careful crafting of the perfect, manipulative lure?

And it had worked. She stood beside her husband's dead body, a suspect, exactly where he wanted her. What, exactly, did he stand to gain?

No sooner had Graham departed for Egypt than Harlowe reappeared in the pub—following a prolonged and conspicuous period of absence. He'd congratulated Julia on her recent marriage, then installed himself at the corner table where he proceeded to hold court. He had a certain charm that rendered him an expert in gathering questionable individuals about him. For a while, he'd abandoned his pseudo-druid friends and focused his attentions on customers, those with deep pockets and interests in all things ancient Egypt.

But, following his recent argument with Marston, the scruffy unkempt mead-drinkers had returned. She frowned. Was it possible the entire group had been involved in plotting against her husband, in orchestrating his death?

What had she missed, distancing herself, spending the bulk of her time in the pub kitchen, baking bread and fussing over her various experimental brews? She only appeared publicly to help at the bar on busy nights. Behavior Marston encouraged. He disliked her conversing with his clients, poking her nose into any of his backroom business deals. Tricky, having a wife with morals.

Most evenings she returned home, slipped up the back stairs into their apartments above the pub to comb through hieroglyphic and cuneiform translations on a hunt for any and all references to beer and bread. By day, she lost herself in the basement laboratories of the British Museum, carefully cultivating and fermenting different yeast varieties, ancient strains that she'd teased from archeological remains under sterile conditions and coaxed back to life. Her aim was to catalogue their alcohol tolerance—the percentage of sugars converted into alcohol and how high she could drive those alcohol levels before the yeast became inactive—along with their preferred temperature and, of course, taste.

Graham tugged at her elbow. A wise woman would heed his not-at-all-subtle direction to exit this macabre scene, but she pulled away. His touch was a painful reminder of what could have been, and she needed to focus on her future.

If she ended up leaving London, the *Tricholoma* pine-mushrooms would provide her with an innovative project to take with her to Oxford. Provided Mr. Black was as good as his word.

If she stayed, however, she intended to offer fairy ring matsutake wine and ale. She imagined an erudite customer base, individuals interested in trying such a novelty along with a selection of beer and bread fashioned from long-lost yeast strains.

"I need my samples." She took a step forward. She wasn't leaving without her basket. Bioluminescent fungi might grow on dead trees, but those produced a green glow. These mushrooms produced a luminescence in a yellow tint that was, as yet, undocumented.

Mr. Black moved to block her progress. "I'm sorry. I can't allow you to disturb the scene any further."

She locked eyes with the agent, welding her vertebrae into a solid column of steel. "For reasons you are well aware, I must insist. These mushrooms are exceedingly rare. The specimens I collected need to be handled properly or I won't be able to—"

"Contemplating Oxford, are you? Very well." Mr. Black closed his eyes for a moment. "Scientists, a plague on my life."

She craned her neck and held her breath as he retrieved her basket and tucked her paper-wrapped glowing mushrooms and the pine saplings inside. He handed it back to her.

The breath she'd been holding whooshed out her lungs in a rush of relief—the specimens within were undamaged.

"Finish sweeping the tombs," Mr. Black ordered. He turned away, tugging a pencil and strip of message paper from a pocket. "Keep Mrs. Marston in your custody at all times."

Her hand tightened on the basket's handle. "What are the odds we'll find more stray bodies?"

"High." Graham's voice was soft. "We have reason to think Marston was conducting a mummy unwrapping party."

"So one body, long dead and desiccated." She kept her voice light, rather hoping Graham would agree.

"Any extras will be quite fresh," he said. "Let's move. It's best if we finish our search before anyone else arrives."

Not what she'd hoped to hear. What had Marston been up to?

This time, she let Graham pull her away, tug her feet into forward movement while she wrapped her mind around the chain of events that had so radically altered today's agenda. Not only today, but the rest of her life. It was simultaneously thrilling and terrifying.

"From the look upon your face, you have specific fresh bodies in mind. Ones with names. Who are we hoping to find still alive and wandering within the cemetery's walls?" Acknowledging the twisting churn of her innards was not an option. She could—would—handle this without squeamishness. Insects and fungi and bodies and death, a common enough quartet. Her stomach would settle. Eventually.

"Why was Marston here, conducting a mummy unwrapping, when his antiquities dealership, though little more than legally sanctioned looting, is ever so much more profitable? And what does all this have to do with your precipitous return to London?"

He certainly hadn't returned for her.

Was that hurt she heard in her own voice, colored by the wistfulness of what-could-have-been threading through her thoughts? It was. She glanced away, hiding a grimace. So much for achieving an attitude of indifference. Unfair, she knew, given he'd proposed on bended knee. She was the one who'd refused to break her engagement with Marston.

"Straight to business, then." His own voice echoed her feelings, tight with unspoken words. "Via the black market, Marston and Harlowe acquired a mummy case, along with other artifacts, from the Theban Necropolis—the west bank opposite Luxor complete with an undisturbed human occupant. Inside the case, a thief hid stolen Egyptian technology. Technology I am tasked with retrieving."

"Which explains why two agents of the Crown are hunting for Professor Marston and guests in Highgate Cemetery as the sun rises. Our government is not overly concerned about the ancient artifacts, amulets and remains in and of themselves."

"All too true. As to who?" He slid her an inquiring look. "Lady Tramontin's son, the new Lord Tramontin, and his wife."

She sighed. "Both of whom have been frequent

customers at The Monocled Raven. As you no doubt well know."

Graham nodded. "She alerted us as to the date of the gathering and we set about watching the pub. We followed Harlowe and, when cornered in his apartments in the early morning hours, he denied any knowledge and, instead, pointed us at Marston, mentioning the professor in the process of conducting an unwrapping."

"Harlowe did?" That drew her up short. "I'd expected his name to be on the list of people for whom we're searching."

"If only." He snorted. "He was careful to cover his arse with an alibi."

"Was he? Did you find them both snug in a bed?" The thought cheered her, the idea of Harlowe's bedsport being interrupted that he might be questioned, bare-arsed and frustrated.

"All but." A faint rumble deep in his chest suggested suppressed laughter. "There was also a clockwork Anubis standing guard outside his building, though he denied ownership."

"Anubis?" She frowned. "Interesting. I've not seen a clockwork jackal about, though there's been a rather rough-looking clockwork dog wandering nearby streets. He's joked about adopting it and naming it Kynan—Welsh for hound."

"Celtic studies, his current field. I was surprised to find Harlowe obsessed with druids."

She nodded. "He's forever bringing me jars of honey and

pressuring me to experiment with mead. And, of late, his scruffy friends have returned."

"Clockwork guard animals are illegal."

"As if that would concern him." She snorted. "Or Marston. If he'd known about the clockwork Anubis, he might well have insisted upon borrowing the clockwork contraption for the unwrapping party, for protection *and* ambiance."

Graham looked thoughtful. "As Harlowe suggested himself while hinting that the professor was conducting a mummy unwrapping in a cemetery. I propose we investigate the Egyptian Avenue. It's as close to the Valley of the Kings as can be managed in London."

"Spine-chilling mystery and blood-curdling drama in the dead of night with men opening a resin-coated coffin to reveal the dead within while torches cast a flickering light across cold tomb walls."

Though the fad had faded somewhat, mummy unwrapping parties were still a draw for *ton* in search of macabre entertainment. Amazing, the ladies and gentlemen who would gasp at the sight of a stockinged ankle or employ a fan when they caught a glimpse of a lace-edged petticoat but thought nothing of gathering close to the dried remains of thousands-of-years-dead corpses to watch as someone unwound strips of linen from their desiccated, bare skin.

Nothing like eliciting the excitement that accompanies the shame and horror of grave robbing in what amounted to an urban garden. Such was convenient and sanitary amusement for the *ton*.

"Alas, there's far more to it than that. The Egyptian technology is being employed to deadly effect. We need to put an end to the deaths by finding and securing the stolen items."

"Which is in the form of a copper clockwork scarab? Implying that Marston and, by extension, Harlowe decided to dabble in international espionage?" Such news failed to surprise her.

"We're not certain." He frowned as they walked side by side upon the packed dirt of the cemetery path. "Marston's attire indicates involvement, and thereby agreement, but his death suggests he was unaware of the full scope of what was included in his purchase." He paused. "Harlowe's convenient absence, on the other hand, suggests he was very aware. I've been chasing this clockwork scarab across Europe for weeks now. In its wake? Dead bodies and insane, raving men."

"This has happened before?" The scope of this investigation was rapidly expanding. The fine hairs on the back of her neck rose. Had she been in imminent danger and utterly oblivious to that fact? "How many times? Where?"

The sun hung higher in the sky now, and the morning mists had begun to burn away. Insects buzzed. Birds chirped. Which only served to highlight and underscore the irritated frown that tugged at Graham's lips, gathering a dark cloud above his head.

"Before I share the rest," he began, "will you tell me everything you remember about the clockwork scarab? I want to hear your unbiased account. I've yet to lay eyes upon the insect myself." He tapped at the wooden handle looped over her wrist. "You tried to catch it with the basket?"

"I *did* catch it." She lifted her chin ever so slightly, proud she'd not screeched and run from an insect. "And it would be in my possession even now, had the creature's attempted escape not landed me on my knees beside Marston's dead body, scaring me half to death." An entirely justifiable response. She slid him a suspicious glance. "Was the contraption responsible for his death, covered in tiny mushrooms as it was?"

"Mushrooms?" His eyebrows climbed high upon his forehead. "That would be new information."

"New?" She frowned. How was it they knew so little of the creature they hunted? "Small fungal bodies covered the entire surface of its metallic carapace."

"Of what kind?"

She shook her head. "The contraption moved too fast and then—well, stumbling upon the dead body of one's husband tends to disturb the logical thought process."

"I imagine so." He snorted, not pretending any reverence for a dead man who had tried to ruin his life.

Not that they themselves had been without guilt.

Feelings between them had been badly wounded when she'd decided to go ahead with her planned marriage to the professor.

Feelings that weren't quite dead. Could they be mended?

She tossed him a sidelong glance, wondering. "Tell me how you, specifically, became involved in this particular investigation. Mr. Black isn't bothered by the... conflict of interest?"

A handful of words that skimmed over their past. Did he wish to renew their acquaintance? He'd given her no indication. She was a widow and free, but with Marston's body still laying in the underbrush it was far too soon. Or, for all she knew, he might be engaged to another woman. Or harbor resentment about how she'd ended things. A sentiment to which he was entitled.

He snorted. "As I've come to know the agent—inasmuch as one can—I begin to believe I was selected with a situation much like this one in mind. A connection to Egyptian antiquities, yet one step removed."

"Selected." She let the word hang between them for a moment. "I imagine there is *some* training involved in becoming a Queen's agent. That you didn't simply holster a weapon and agree to chase after any villains at which he pointed?"

"Truthfully? You've rather struck the nail on the head." His admission emerged on a grumble. "After my banishment from the British Museum..." Heat rose to stain his cheeks. Anger? Embarrassment? Both? "The Rankine Institute was loathe to let me return. As such, I made inquiries at the Lister Institute, proposing the use of cathode ray fluorescence to study Egyptian mummies in a manner that would eliminate the need to unwrap them. I first met Mr. Black when I arrived for my interview. He'd heard of my troubles and offered to rubber stamp my research provided I agreed to be eyes and ears for him inside Egypt's borders, to act if the occasion should arise."

"Which it has," she pointed out. Paused. Then decided to state the obvious. "Rather impossible not to note that your investigation is focused upon those against whom you carry a grudge."

"I expected you might take offense." He spoke the words with a tight jaw. "Which is why I objected when Mr. Black wanted me to renew our old acquaintance."

A direct blow to her heart. One she deserved.

Her throat constricted. Did he despise her, blame her for his exile? Though she'd had nothing to do with the accusations leveled at him, their intimate relationship—one she'd initiated —had provoked Marston's baser instincts causing him to assert his dominance through underhanded and extreme means.

She'd had no right to drag Graham into the turmoil of her life.

To seal their engagement, Professor Marston had dropped an enthusiastic kiss upon her lips. A chill had run through her, straight to her feet, freezing them to the ground. Marriage to a man twice her age held no appeal and she knew then her agreement was a mistake. But there could be no backing out. Without that marriage, there would be no settling her father's gambling debts. The pub would fail and debt collectors would arrive, tossing her family out into the streets without two coins to rub together.

Which was when her mind frantically cast about for a way to calm the inner voice that screamed and cried out, begging that she not throw herself on a pyre, that she not sacrifice herself for something as mundane as beer and bread.

Commodities, her logical brain had replied, which sustained life. Both financially as a business and personally as an academic pursuit. If she failed to marry satisfactorily, both ended. Abruptly.

She'd ruthlessly silenced her misgivings and focused on addressing one particular experience she expected to be denied once vows were spoken: pleasure.

Years working alongside an overwhelming majority of male colleagues had provided her with a treasure trove of cerebral information as concerned sexual activity. And exactly zero practical experience. She'd been curious. And apprehensive. The professor was a selfish man—attentiveness to a wife in the marriage bed seemed unlikely. Which was why she'd propositioned Graham. Someone she trusted, someone the ladies fell over backward to attract. Someone who wouldn't grow attached.

Or so she'd thought.

Her mistake.

She'd suffered the consequences ever since and, once more, would pay the price.

They followed the right fork in the path, toward the ancient Cedar of Lebanon that towered over the catacombs of the Egyptian Avenue, over the tops of the tombs tucked into its roots.

"Mr. Black believes Harlowe is the man behind this theft, not my former husband?"

Amazing how quickly she'd slid into use of past tense verbs, how readily she looked forward to donning dull black and taking full control of the pub. No one would dare argue with the changes she intended to implement, not while she was in mourning. Of course, that presumed she was not locked behind bars, her rights stripped away by a formal accusation of murder.

"He does now. Marston's name might have been on the packing slip, and he certainly wasn't innocent, but it's Harlowe who has the need to make a name for himself, who has the nerve to entangle himself in espionage. And it might have worked, but for my off-the-books efforts on behalf of the Crown."

"A most effective maneuver to avoid working for any stuffed shirts *and* continue studying faience Egyptian mummy amulets."

His current job meant he would work in a different building in an entirely different neighborhood of London, saving her the pain of catching glimpses of him bent over a specimen, cravat loose and askew. Sleeves rolled above elbows. Hair tousled. He'd changed little during his time abroad, save his sun-kissed skin had acquired a temporary golden tone and his crooked smile now prompted crinkles at the corners of his eyes. She found herself rather fond of them.

Had he removed his shirt in the field? A captivating thought. Graham hot and sweaty, coated with the dust and dirt of an archeological dig, his trousers pulling tight as he bent over to—

She tore her gaze away. Such fantasies would do her no good. Pondering the intricacies of personal intimacies within the confines of an expedition tent was a mental exercise best left untouched. Especially as it only fueled speculation about the women—yes, plural—who might have been lucky enough to share that private space with him.

Before them, the twin obelisks of the Egyptian gateway stabbed into the sky, flanking the columns and arches designed to recall the sepulchral temples at Thebes and mark the entrance to the many tombs that lined the Street of the Dead.

"Working for the Crown comes with many benefits," he said. "You were offered a similar escape?"

"I was."

Leaving the British Museum would have risked her husband's ire. But Mr. Black's offer had been tempting. Again she shook her head at the verb tense her mind chose. *Had.* Leaving London for a position at Oxford no longer held any appeal. Not if she could continue her work at the British Museum unimpeded. Studying bioluminescent pine-mushrooms would serve as an amusing hobby, a curiosity that she might leverage to draw long-ago customers back into The Monocled Raven.

Cart before the clockwork horse.

Graham might be back in London and she might be a lusty, unsatisfied widow with inappropriate thoughts of the romantic variety, but Marston was dead and she was currently the top suspect. A fact of which she needed to keep reminding herself. How could Graham possibly be interested in rekindling their relationship? Especially after she'd left him to marry another man.

"You declined?"

"Not exactly. I was reluctant to abandon The Monocled Raven before fully understanding the situation or the nature of the man or his offer."

"You asked questions?" A note of alarm crept into his voice. "About Mr. Black?"

"Those of us in the hospitality business have connections." She slid him a look, letting the corners of her mouth turn up into a knowing grin as they passed into the shadow cast by the stone arch of the Egyptian gateway. "Not that it didn't take some digging, but there are quite a few fascinating, if unsubstantiated, whispers about events in which his involvement can neither be confirmed nor denied. Then today of all days, I find myself face to carapace with a clockwork scarab sprouting tiny mushrooms. Seconds later, the elusive Mr. Black arrives on scene with you hot on his heels. Leaving me with even more questions."

"Such questions can have deadly consequences."

Her amusement fell away. "So it appears."

CHAPTER SIX

He and Black had been searching the foliage along the cemetery's paths as they made their way to the Egyptian Gate, sweeping the gleam of decil-amps over the wild tangle, all in hopes of catching a ray of light glinting off copper. But for Julia's cry, they would have passed by her luminous fairy ring unaware of the dead man's presence. Worse—though he harshly judged the value of a human life—they would not have known the clockwork scarab wandered loose upon the grounds.

Graham had been so certain they would find both inside one of the cemetery's larger tombs. Something, it seemed, had gone wrong.

Or was that right?

Harlowe had, after all, led them on a merry chase, keeping all attention focused on him allowing his mentor to slip out somehow in the dark hours of the morning. Professor Marston had been set up. It only remained to be determined if his death was an orchestrated outcome or a happy accident. How long, he wondered, had his body lain undiscovered in the undergrowth?

The woman he loved was a widow. Every last ounce of his willpower had been required to not let the deep satisfaction that simple fact brought him show upon his face.

When she'd invited herself into his bed nearly a year past, he ought to have turned her away, to have resisted his longing and preserved his honor. But she'd been forthright and direct about her reasons—and thoughts of the professor introducing her to bedroom activities had turned his stomach. Worse, he'd thought he might convince her to abandon her engagement, to marry him instead.

He'd badly misjudged the situation.

Once this was over, following a brief period of mourning, they would be free to marry. Openly and without shame.

But not until they solved the mystery of her husband's death. Which involved locating and catching that damn clockwork scarab and finding evidence to pin its theft on Harlowe. He wanted nothing more than to see the slippery bastard discredited and denied all further access to archeological sites and materials. Graham wouldn't object if they threw him in prison.

Most of all, he wanted the man cut off from ever approaching Julia again.

Their rivalry always circled back to her.

Harlowe's nature was, at its core, mercenary. Had he caught wind of her questions and decided his heart's desire was far more trouble than she was worth and set her up as a murder suspect? Possibly. Or perhaps a damsel in distress was exactly what he wanted. If he'd been truly worried, Harlowe would have contrived for Julia to accompany her husband to the mummy unwrapping and ensured her own body would even now lay beside the professor's in the cemetery undergrowth.

But knowing that she'd asked *questions* about Black sent a shiver down his spine. Digging into the background of a high-ranking spy seeking answers that not even his fellow agents could answer? Never a good idea. Alerting Harlowe to the possibility that she might be cooperating with authorities? Even worse.

Cursing under his breath, he grabbed her wrist and spun about to face her. She bumped up against his chest yet made no effort to step away.

The scent of toasted bread, sweet cream and honey met his nose. An aroma he'd come to associate with morning Julia, with the woman who'd risen from his bed—where they'd spent the night with their limbs tangled between rumpled sheets—to sneak over to his hearth with a toasting fork and a kettle of water. If there'd been crumbs on the mattress, he'd not noticed, intent as he'd been upon licking drops of honey from her soft skin.

Here, in this patch of bright light, his gaze locked with hers. "What do I need to do to impress upon you that you cannot be asking those kinds of questions?"

"I was discreet," she huffed. "And how am I to make a critical decision about my future, knowing next to nothing? A mysterious man walks into the bar and claims to work for the Duke of Avesbury. Insists he knows everything about me. Asks me to betray my husband for the greater good when all risk is to be mine and not his."

A sound argument. "I'll protect—"

"Empty promises," she interrupted, rolling her eyes. "You have an alibi. Harlowe has an alibi. While I was, as always, alone."

Though her tone was matter of fact, his heart ached at the statement, even though she had chosen a marriage of convenience that saved her ungrateful father from debtor's prison and her sisters from penury. "Which is why I have no intention of letting you stand before a magistrate."

"An offer that brings us back to the task set before us." Her hand fell upon his waistcoat. She made no effort to push him away. "Do I have this correct? Find the missing Egyptian antiquities to locate some stolen device called an inquisitor? This contraption will somehow allow us to locate the clockwork scarab that we might examine its inner workings and determine what, precisely, led to Marston's death?"

"Close," he replied. "Very close."

And indeed they were. Pressed together from hip to thigh, her mouth inches from his own. A kiss was entirely inappropriate given their situation. But when had improper behavior ever stopped them?

"You've been away eleven months and seventeen days." Her palm flattened above the rapid thump of his heart while his chest rose and fell, lungs struggling to extract enough oxygen from the suddenly too-thin air. "So unless you're going to kiss me, we ought to turn our attention to the tombs."

"Is that what you want?" For it was precisely what he wished to do. That and so much more. "Here and now?"

She glanced away, a guarded look shuttering her face. "Is there someone else? Or do you find it impossible to forgive my choices?"

"There's no one else," he answered. Never would be. "Your family, are they well?"

She nodded. "Betsy married a solicitor, Alice a banker, and Father set off upon an adventure to find new opportunities in South Africa."

"And now you own the pub outright, while I am gainfully employed."

"Why, Mr. Leyburn!" Julia tilted her head. "Do you wish to renew your attentions?" The beginnings of a coy smile tugged at her lips.

Unwilling to match the sweet lightness she attempted here among tall trees and stones, he kept his voice somber. "With the intention to marry," he clarified. "What I want is for the banns to be called as soon as this unpleasant business is behind us. My terms this time, not yours."

Her lips parted on a soft exhale. "Is that a proposal?"

Was it?

Much as he did not wish the day of the professor's death to be the day they pledged their lives to each other, he wanted his intentions clear.

"Yes." He dipped his head, breathing the words against her ear, reveling in the soft catch of her silky hair against his stubbled cheek. "With a brief engagement, so as not to skip entirely the pleasures of rediscovering who you are, who *we* are."

He dropped his hand to her waist, curled his fingers into the fabric gathered there until he could feel the bones of her corset beneath. Judging from the rapid flutter of the pulse at her neck, she found the notion more than agreeable.

"That sounds lovely," she whispered back. Her arms rose, wrapped about his neck. Fingertips played with the curl of hair at his nape. "I wouldn't mind an arm always on offer, a hand at the small of my back when we enter a room—but no physical affection of the indecent sort. I am, after all, a very new widow." Her lips curved upward. "Unless we're very much alone."

"Alone? Such as pausing during an outdoor stroll to take in the scenery." He let his gaze sweep over her face, dropping only briefly to admire her cleavage. "Now, for example."

"Exactly." She turned her head, brushing her lips across his, waking long-sleeping nerve endings. "I wonder, can you still deliver a kiss that will curl my toes?" Her words were a challenge, delivered a moment before the soft press of her lips against his own drove all rational thought from his head.

Challenge accepted.

He pulled her from the path, seeking a bit of shaded privacy beneath a tree, and pinned her between its trunk and his body, wanting her to know exactly how much she affected him. With a finger beneath her chin, he tipped her face upward and kissed her in a manner that was anything but chaste or respectable. Parting her lips with the sweep of his tongue, he poured forth long-suppressed desires and renewed promises.

When she melted against him on a soft whimper, a world of possibilities exploded into a riot of color. It had been so long. So very, very long. When she'd let him walk away, he'd been a shell of a man, a dried husk, an automaton with every stray thought colored in sepia tones. Travel and life in Egypt had begun to revive him—it was a fascinating land after all—but not all of him had revived. Not until this very moment.

All lingering doubts evaporated like morning mist. Everything had changed and yet nothing had changed. Mutual attraction was not at all in question.

He trailed his fingertips—ones he knew were rough from digging in the dirt and sand—over the smooth, soft rise of her breast. She gasped her pleasure into his mouth and he rewarded her with yet more friction, sliding his hand behind and beneath the fabric of her bodice, cupping her breast to circle the tight bud with the pad of his thumb.

The groan that emerged from deep in her throat sent hot, pleasurable anticipation rushing though him. All of it edged with the sharp ache of need. He had the sudden, intense desire to hitch her up onto a gravestone and reach for the hem of her skirt.

Sinking deep inside her would satisfy them both and cement their reunion, but he couldn't—not here, not with his colleague nearby and more agents on the way. That would cross the line into indecent.

And there was the not-so-small problem of Harlowe who continued to enjoy freedom. The man would do his best to throw a wrench into any plans they crafted. Plans he was more determined than ever to see through to fruition.

He broke their kiss and stared down into her eyes. Eyes that were dark with aching desire. "And? Have your toes curled?"

"You've left me weak-kneed and wobbly. And from the feel of you, I'm not the only one left muddle-headed." Her lips twitched with humor. "That hard length of an iron key in your pocket pressed against my hip. Does it open doors to spaces more private than the one we currently occupy? I don't suppose you know any... unoccupied tombs?"

Her words sent fire racing down his spine and flames dancing through his blood. A moment ago, he would have thought it impossible for his cock to grow any harder. The impulse to acquiesce, to haul her behind the first door he could unlock nearly broke his fraying resolve.

She'd let him. He was certain of it.

Once or twice inside the British Museum, they'd stolen away from their studies into the dusty, shadowed corners of a room devoted to the storage of pottery shards to enjoy each other's company in the most indecent, if satisfying, manner.

But that was then and this was now.

He'd have her promises first.

Ignoring his body's roar of protest, he dragged his lips along the edge of her jawline, nipping delicate skin behind her ear. "Tempting. But I know of no such tomb." He stepped back, slowly and with much regret, taking in the sounds of birdsong and leaves that rustled in the morning breeze "Besides, you've yet to agree."

"You've yet to propose." Her hands slid from his shoulders to his chest.

"Both true."

"Should it matter," the crook of her finger caught his waistband, anchoring him in place, "it's been months since Marston last attempted consummation."

His fingers tightened on her hips. "You never..."

She gave a small shake of her head. "Annulment remained an option until—" She waved a hand back toward the tunnel through which they'd passed. "Well, until I found him beside the fairy circle."

Graham had been her first and her last.

That ought not thrill him as it did, but what man wished to learn another man was in the regular habit of slipping between the sheets with the woman he loved? Still, from the look on her face, there had been attempts at consummation. While he'd been baking in the Saharan sun free to pursue his career, she'd been trapped here in the damp and dark, coping with the sharp fragments of her life—conducting research during the day while bartending and appeasing an arrogant archaeologist at night.

"I won't pretend I'm disappointed," he admitted, stepping backward. Her hand fell away. Cool morning air rushed between them. A necessity to clear his head. "About his frustrations or his death. I am sorry at what you must have endured."

"I agreed to the marriage, honored my vows." She lifted a shoulder. "For the most part, he left me alone, confining his jealousy to casting dark stares at any men who dared approach me, so long as I turned a blind eye to his back-room sales."

"No marriage agreement includes implicit agreement to assist one's spouse with illegal activity."

"Which is why I intended to aid Mr. Black." She frowned and tugged the neckline of her bodice back into place. "A situation that has unfortunately escalated." Julia slid past him, returning to the path. "How is this clockwork scarab responsible for Marston's convenient, if untimely, demise? And how does stealing a mechanical beetle count as international espionage? Everyone knows that if you visit Clockwork Corridor with enough coins in your purse, you can walk away with marvelous contraptions of Romani construction."

Time to place all his cards on the table.

"We don't know how it kills, not exactly."

She blinked. "And yet you're pursuing it? Perhaps you ought to start at the beginning?"

His thoughts exactly.

He nodded. "I've yet to lay eyes on the device myself but am instead following a string of events that began in Luxor. A group of wealthy tourists from the continent had traveled up the Nile aboard their dahabeeyah to visit the Valley of the Kings. The boat, heading back to Cairo, was charged with conveying a shipment of artifacts from a season's excavations. All common enough practices. But the night it departed, innovative technology was stolen from the Ptah Institute."

"Not so much a coincidence, I assume?"

"Correct." He nodded. "Yet the events were unconnected at the time. Later, during their voyage, our tourists threw a wild party that ended in shame and humiliation for some. While events were contained to the boat and did not spill into the local populace..." He slid her an expectant look.

"The rumors, nonetheless, winged their way to shore?" She snorted.

"Just so." He recalled the mocking comments whispered in Arabic that he'd overheard in the market. "After a night of debauchery that ended in drugged and drunken nudity, a number of the party never made it to their beds, instead sleeping on the deck well into late morning. Not much in the way of linen clothing was involved. Skin never before exposed to the sun adorned only with ancient Egyptian pectorals, wide bracelets and the occasional ring present gossip-worthy sunburn patterns."

"I can only imagine." Her eyes were wide, her mouth open. "And this is when the clockwork scarab first made its appearance?"

He nodded. "The device was described as a wonder brought aboard by a Bedouin for a night's amusement, flying among the attendees and delighting all. As it was—at the time—unconnected with the technology theft, its existence was dismissed as nothing more than a rich man's toy. Until another gathering ended with a woman's death, then the clockwork scarab was blamed and revelers described how a Bedouin by the name of Saleh was able to call the mechanical insect to his side."

"Called to his side?" she repeated. "How is such a thing possible?"

"Easily enough, as he turned out to be the scientist who designed—and absconded with—the syntholink and its paired tethersync inquisitor."

"Syntholink?" Her eyebrows drew together. "Tethersync inquisitor?"

"They're two components that work together. A latent transponder programed to respond to a specific circular polarization interrogating signal with a temporal—"

She held up a hand, interrupting. "The physics of the stolen technology are lost upon me."

He tried again. "We're looking for a broadcasting device that sends out a signal asking where its other half is located. The other half answers, allowing the person in possession of the broadcasting device to track it."

Her brow furrowed. "And how big is this... inquisitor?"

He used his hands to shape a box roughly the size of a loaf of bread.

"And the syntholink?"

"No larger than the tip of your little finger."

"And capable of fitting inside the clockwork scarab?"

"Precisely." He took a deep breath. "We believe the Bedouin scientist has modified the clockwork device so that, when the syntholink receives the signal, the insect responds in a pre-coded patterned behavior that returns it to the inquisitor."

"Much like a skeet pigeon, carrying a message to a predetermined location."

"Exactly." Julia was always a swift study. "Save the destination is mobile and capable of calling the scarab from a distance, instructing it to spread its wings and fly to the source of the signal. A retrieval mechanism, if you will."

Her jaw dropped. "No wonder the Ptah Institute—Egypt—wants its stolen technology returned. This is groundbreaking communications behavior."

He held up a finger. "There's more. Imagine planting such a device as a clockwork scarab, one with assassination instructions, but possessing the ability to remotely retrieve it from the scene of the crime."

She pressed a hand to her heart. "You believe that's what Harlowe did to Marston?"

"I can't rule it out."

"Back to your story." She flapped a hand. "Rumors of these claims reach official ears. I gather this is when you received a cryptic telegram from one Mr. Black instructing you to give chase?"

He laughed. "Close enough. Agent Hassan, my Egyptian counterpart, and I were tasked with locating this Saleh and his clockwork scarab, but the trail went cold in Alexandria. For a while we cast about, turning over rocks. While we found plenty of insects, it wasn't until a strange report from Sardinia reached our ears that we knew he was on the move. British tourists—"

"Let me guess. Dressed in Egyptian garb?"

"Spot on," he answered. "A woman wearing a bead-net dress over a linen sheath danced into a hotel lobby, raving about the coming of the horned god while clutching the silver ankh that hung about her neck. One that ought to have been packed carefully away with the other antiquities in a certain shipment from Luxor."

"Interesting. Reports of depraved orgies. Drunken or drugged individuals. And then a link to ancient Egyptian gods." She tapped her chin. "Horned gods are common in many cultures and their worship often involves fertility and virility. If we narrow considerations to Egypt, one god occasionally depicted with ram's horns is Ammon-Ra."

His step hitched as he glanced at her sideways. "A bit outside your area of expertise, gods and goddess."

"Hardly," she huffed. "I've learned much, listening behind the bar. The best way to sell an antiquity to a reluctant buyer? Link it to a god or a goddess. Convince the customer that owning such a relic will confer traits or unlock powers associated with that deity. Wallets open and purse strings loosen."

"I see your point." He resumed walking. She'd hit the nail on the head. "Unfortunately, when we located the host of her party, the guests had fled, not wanting to serve as witnesses when a man had died."

"Died?" Her voice climbed into a new octave.

"Egyptian garb. Found collapsed and unresponsive, dying soon thereafter."

"With mention of a foreign man in possession of a clockwork scarab?"

"And dressed as a high priest. The host had hired him to roam among his guests, just another curiosity to enhance the atmosphere of an Egyptian-themed event. We left the island, following vague reports of an Arab headed north to Corsica and chased Saleh and his clockwork scarab across Europe for weeks. In his wake? More dead bodies and insane, raving men and women. When we caught the Bedouin at the port of Calais, he refused to speak, but we found a bill of lading pointing at none other than your husband."

"Former husband," she corrected, her lips pulling into a frown. "But we both know he carefully stayed on the correct side of international law. Which is one of the many reasons you suspect that Harlowe," she ground out the name, "managed to convince Marston to dabble in international espionage?"

"The professor had everything he wanted."

She slanted him a look.

"Save an heir." He sighed, acknowledging Marston's apparent impotence. "Harlowe is unmarried and nothing more than an assistant. He's also lazy and opportunistic. Why break free and begin anew when you can stage a coup? He need only set Marston on a disastrous path, alibi himself, and deny, deny, deny. I've little doubt Harlowe actively courted the import of this particular mechanical beetle specifically so that he could introduce the professor to the Order of the Winged Scarab."

CHAPTER SEVEN

"A cult?" Julia drew up short and gaped. "One dedicated to Khepri?"

Though not a horned god, when depicted in human form, the entirety of the insect became the Egyptian god's face with the forelegs of the beetle projecting above the head, not unlike horns. A hallucinating, possibly drugged, woman could be forgiven her mistake.

"So it would appear," Graham answered.

Her dead husband worshiping the scarab-faced god? *Worshiping?* Her mind immediately and loudly rejected the possibility as preposterous. Improbable. Far-fetched. Marston had placed no one above him and that included gods and goddesses from *any* religion.

And yet, here they were. In a graveyard. His activities under investigation—his death as well.

Before their marriage, she would have dismissed the possibility that Marston would involve himself in anything that smacked of religion. Yet a shared living space had brought her new insight into the man's quiet obsessions and his willingness to sweep aside morality to achieve his aims. Why not also logic?

No, that last part she found hard to believe. Unless there was something to be gained by pretending, if in exchange he received something very tangible and self-serving?

Yes. She had to admit he might well trek into a graveyard after midnight and don a linen skirt to... What exactly remained to be determined.

No, that was wrong. Heat rose to her face. Drunken nakedness. Fertility. His determination to finally consummate their marriage.

But how could this Order of the Winged Scarab make promises of curing his impotence?

"Marston would have thought this cult's ceremonies nothing but theatrical nonsense." Julia pondered the situation aloud. "A little something to add a dramatic flair to the dusty and tired traditions associated with a mummy unwrapping. Yes, he'd have gone along with the cultlike ritual if he thought it would sell more antiquities."

"I'm certain that contributed." Graham didn't sound any more convinced than she felt.

There was more to this, and she had the sinking feeling sex and drugs were the driving force behind this cult's activities with the mummy unwrapping merely an excuse to gather.

She let out a long, slow exhale. "Remind me of Khepri's significance?" All she could recall was that scarab beetles made it a habit of pushing large balls of dung across the ground in which they'd laid their eggs.

"He's a solar deity, god of the morning sun," he said. "Responsible every dawn for rolling the newly reborn sun across the sky. A god of rebirth and renewal." Graham cleared his throat, slid her a look. "About Marston's impotence..."

Julia groaned. There was no avoiding the topic. Theirs had been a misery of a marriage bed. So much effort, so much embarrassment and humiliation for them both. Marston had placed himself on strange and strict diets, consumed an array of questionable substances, smeared his male member with lotions and ointments. He'd even tried mild electric stimulation. Nothing had worked.

Obsessed with power, Marston hadn't been content unless he was in the topmost position of power, dominant. With his career approaching legend and the increasing financial success in antiquities, he lacked but one thing—proof of his virility. Several other establishments in various locations might have served as a clearinghouse for his antiquities, but marriage to Julia served another purpose—to remove the bright, young female student beyond the reach of other Egyptologists. She was the gilded feather in his cap, lacking a single feature: a belly rounded with his child.

Had his inability to perform combined with the knowledge that Graham, his protégé, had once warmed her bed been the fulcrum upon which Harlowe propped his lever to prod his mentor, his supervisor into chasing after this new, dubious solution? Had this clockwork scarab and whatever drug it provided offered him a chance to renew his visits to her bed after months of absence?

Resentment for her dead husband stirred deep in her gut, dark and oily.

When she'd first learned his funds arrived in their bank account via the black market, she'd objected. But his threats had trumped hers. If she breathed so much as a word, he promised to divorce her. Publicly. Ending her academic career while keeping The Monocled Raven as his own.

Why, yes, her husband had commented, he was well aware of her premarital indiscretions—why else would he delay consummation but to ensure no cuckoo egg landed in his nest? A calm statement that had made her break out in a cold sweat. Only when time had proven she'd not conceived Graham's child had Marston begun to visit her bed. Frustrating as his attempts at claiming his marital rights had been, it had placed them on equal footing. Both were motivated to keep each other's secrets.

That he'd sought to renew his attempts did not make his death her fault.

She banished such thoughts and, instead, rolled her eyes. "Oh, for aether's sake. Are you telling me this cult claimed to possess a cure? A ritual that would restore his flagging member?"

"We're not certain," he admitted. "Min, the god sporting an erect phallus with a cult devoted to fertility and sexual potency, would have made more sense for that particular goal. But instead we're chasing after a winged scarab representing the god Khepri."

"Which explains the sudden increase in women patronizing The Monocled Raven." She cast her eyes upward toward the cloudless, blue sky. It was a beautiful morning, a peaceful setting, but they were surrounded by death even as they hunted for a mobile icon of rebirth. She closed her eyes for a moment, swore, then began walking once more. "So much for it being only about the jewelry."

They passed beneath the archway into the Egyptian Avenue and Julia found herself watching for a glint of copper in the slanted morning light that reached into the long tunnel lined by tombs.

What were their chances of happening upon the scarab? Better now that they moved into shadows. Given the fungus growing upon its back, she rather thought the creature would avoid direct sunlight. Beetles as a whole were inclined to crawl into dark, quiet, hidden places. In a graveyard, there were many such opportunities. Yet the creature was not entirely alive, not in a biological sense. Leaving her to wonder at the chances it would choose one of the tombs beside them.

"Jewelry?"

"Women accompanying men, all of them wearing beadwork necklaces strung with funerary amulets once tucked among and within mummy wrappings, the kind said to be imbued with the power of magical rites and spells. Chief among them, the heart scarab symbol of rebirth and renewal."

"Pectorals with a centerpiece featuring a winged scarab holding aloft a sun disc?"

"Yes, much like the one Marston wore." Her fingers tightened into a death grip about the basket handle. "As was the one he gifted me last night. I was to wear it and wait for him in our bed." She huffed. "Sex. Of course it's about sex."

He snorted. "Making the back storage room inadequate for a cult meeting. Hard to imbue a ceremony with magic and mysticism in such an environment."

"It makes a twisted amount of sense, I suppose, to remove to the section of a cemetery with an Egyptian flair to conduct ceremonies. The occupants are certainly in no position to object to the use of their space. Nighttime gatherings would also provide more privacy, especially if—as we suspect—personal intimacy might be involved."

"While I cannot personally confirm such activities are involved," Graham spread his hands wide, "it seems likely. As we followed the Bedouin, we kept encountering the phrase 'kiss of the scarab'."

"Kiss?" Her eyebrows rose. "Does not such an activity require lips, a feature possessed by no arthropod? Could that be a faulty translation of the word 'bite'? Or is that a privilege afforded the high priest acting as the god's representative during ceremonies, the right to kiss whomever he so chooses?"

"That would entice many a man to join the priesthood." Graham rubbed his chin, fighting back a crooked smile. "But no. From what we pieced together, the clockwork scarab will fly to each supplicant in turn, perhaps to land upon their shoulder, whereupon the contraption offers them a kiss. One, it seems, laced with some form of hallucinogen.

No agent has yet to lay eyes upon this device—you're the first."

Julia smiled, amused at the idea of herself as a Queen's agent. On the other hand, she was currently hunting a deadly creature that a foreign country desperately wanted returned. "Could it be a biomech contraption, laboratory enhanced?"

"How did you—" Graham's head whipped about, his focus upon her knife-sharp, all concentration unsoftened with any hint of romance. His eyes narrowed. "While researching Mr. Black, I presume?"

"I heard something about an octopus in Scotland that wasn't entirely biological." She lifted a shoulder, neither confirming nor denying. Was that not what agents did? "In our situation, this scarab isn't entirely mechanical. Copper glinting in the morning light caught my eye, as did the flashes of Egyptian blue, but its carapace was studded with the fruiting bodies of a fungus."

He tipped his head. "What kind?"

"Of fungus?" She poked him in the side and rolled her eyes. "Please. You ascribe to me far too much skill. There was time for only the briefest of glances before it scrambled into the undergrowth then launched itself into the sky with a decided mechanical whir. So do you—or others—think the creature might be alive, at least partially?"

He laughed. "Only you would classify a mechanized mushroom-scarab amalgamation as 'partially alive'. You might be on to something, however; many mushrooms possess hallucinogenic properties, do they not? Like that white-spotted red mushroom Alice encounters during her adventures in Wonderland, the one the hooka-smoking caterpillar sits upon?"

One of her favorite stories. "Where a small nibble on one side of the mushroom will make her grow taller or shorter, depending upon where she nibbles."

"Which side?" he prompted.

"'As it was perfectly round, she found this a very difficult question.'" She quoted, then laughed. "Quite pretty, the fly agaric mushroom. *Amanita muscaria*. And, yes, its toxins are psychoactive. Many report out-of-body experiences and synesthesia. They will not, however, kill a human. What I saw sprouting from the scarab's metallic carapace were tiny mushroom-like structures."

"And yet?"

She shook her head. "It all happened so fast. My expertise is yeast. From there, I leap to mythological and edible mushrooms. I'd need to take a much closer look."

"Then we'd best get on with it." He stopped before the door of a tomb and tugged her close, dropping a slow, soft kiss upon her lips that had her remembering the feel of his unshaven face as it moved over her bare flesh. "I've missed having you in my bed. Badly."

"A sentiment I most definitely return."

"But most of all, I've missed our wandering and bizarre conversations. Of Egyptian gods and mummified remains. Of traditional methods of brewing beer and fermenting wine." He nudged the basket she held. "I'm looking forward to hearing about your plans to concoct a glowing potable drink of the alcoholic variety from mushrooms."

He leaned down and caught her lips again, returning to a slower, more thoughtful kiss. A kiss that promised her everything, including a future together.

The last time he'd kissed her, it had been a goodbye. A broken-hearted farewell. Her father's debt had mushroomed to such enormous proportions she could not afford to turn her back on Marston's offer and choose love, choose a fourth son without current funds or any hope of an inheritance. Few could compete with the accumulated resources of an older man who hobnobbed with the *ton*.

Graham had conceded his losses and stepped aside. If not gracefully.

Her status as a married woman freed her to pursue her studies, particularly within the museum's walls. But even as her altered rank garnered her respect, it also left her very much alone. Few dared to share anything resembling camaraderie when—or so they assumed—a stray comment might find its way to the ear of the department head.

Ought she be riddled with guilt at the thought of throwing herself into the arms of her first and only love while her husband's body still lay in the underbrush? Before she'd been officially cleared of any wrongdoing? Perhaps. Yet the very idea of pretending to be a grieving widow turned her stomach. Theirs had not been a happy marriage and she refused to pretend sorrow for a man who had thought of her as an object to be largely ignored unless she served a purpose to further his own goals.

Inconvenient, and almost annoying, of Marston to die in such a manner. On the other hand, this small adventure, a treasure hunt of sorts, wasn't the worst manner in which to renew acquaintances. After Graham had departed, she'd mentally plucked her heart from her chest and stuffed it in the equivalent of a canonic jar, where it slowly dried and shriveled, no longer of any use for her on this mortal plane. Now she found she still had use of it, that the organ wasn't as desiccated and unresponsive as she'd thought. Instead, it pounded in her chest, pumping blood to all-but-forgotten regions of her anatomy.

Not that he seemed inclined to take things any further than a kiss. Not while working. And, she'd wager, Harlowe would not be content to lay abed with his alibi. No, he would have plans. Plans that needed to be thwarted.

She touched her ungloved fingertips to the scruff that edged his jaw. Ran them across the column of his neck, over the wool of his coat, until they touched upon the seam of the pocket into which he'd tucked the iron key. Not without regret, she pulled it free and stepped away, holding the key between them.

"The sooner we clear our names, the sooner..." She trailed off with a coy smile.

He lifted an eyebrow. "The banns can be called?"

She swatted his chest. "There's no need to rush to the altar to accomplish what's on both our minds."

He laughed, but not convincingly so.

She'd hurt him before. Did he worry she would do so again?

"I'm sorry," she said. "For the way I treated you. It was wrong of me to—"

He pressed a finger to her lips. "Promise not to do it again? To not leave me out in the cold, alone, without offering an explanation?"

She nodded. "Promise."

"That's settled then. Care to do the honors?" He waved a hand toward the door of the tomb, smiling.

She slotted the key into the keyhole and twisted. An echoing thud sounded as it turned, retracting its bolt. At her push, the door groaned an objection before reluctantly granting them entrance.

Graham stepped forward, tugging a decilamp from a pocket. He gave it a shake, then directed the beam of light within. She rose onto her toes, dropping a hand onto his shoulder to peer into the dark.

And saw nothing but shadows cast by shelves holding lead-lined coffins. Not a thing appeared out of place and nothing extraneous caught her eye. Graham swept the flagstone floor with the blue-white beam, revealing nothing more than one might expect—beetles and spiders and a single white moth. No coppery-blue, fungus-topped scarab crawled among them.

He stepped inside the dusty room and turned his attention to the shelves that formed cubbyholes on the walls, providing resting space for a dozen individuals. Which puzzled her until she recalled that the inquisitor they searched for was about the size of a loaf of bread.

"All but one slot is—er—occupied." She closed her eyes

and sent up a prayer to whatever god or goddess might be listening. "Please tell me we do not need to look inside each coffin." Prying lids off coffins less than three thousand years old had never been on her to-do list.

"Aether, no." He sounded as horrified as she felt. "Touch the sides of the coffins. Use your ears. If the inquisitor's orienter is engaged, the chemical battery powering the device may produce warmth. Possibly a clicking sound. Also look for evidence that the tomb hosted a number of recent visitors."

Not at all keen, she followed suit and pressed fingertips to the tops of one coffin after another.

"All cold to the touch?" he asked.

"Yes." She released the breath she'd been holding. Nothing beyond cool, varnished wood. A relief. If only momentary. Yet finding nothing failed to further their aim.

Fitting, how her lighthearted, folkloric-centered attempt at a research project involving a fairy ring had taken a dark turn. She'd been lured to a cemetery and, though she'd not voluntarily stepped within the circle, she'd certainly been drawn into a merry dance, chasing after a poisonous clockwork creature. Pixie-led. Would it end in madness? Would she perish from exhaustion?

Key in hand, they moved to the next vault door. Then the next.

Over and again, they encountered much the same. With a thunk and a creak, the heavy iron doors along the Egyptian Avenue opened, one after the next, all with interiors devoid of incriminating evidence.

They stepped from the shadows cast by the decaying, arched roof of the avenue and into the morning light. Before them lay the Circle of Lebanon, named after the giant tree that stretched its branches overhead. A sunken pathway curved around it, with the twenty catacombs of the inner circle tucked into the earth among the roots. More tombs with Egyptian motifs waiting to be opened and investigated.

"Where to start?" Graham asked. "Inner ring or outer ring?"

"Please." She snorted. "Marston would only cooperate if he could be a member of the inner ring."

CHAPTER EIGHT

"Truer words have never been spoken," Graham replied. "Harlowe only need ensure that something unique about the headdress, the pectoral, the arm bands—any part of the costume worn by the high priest—marked him as the target."

"Is such a thing possible?" The expression upon her face was astonishment mixed with amazement and tinged with worry.

"Not with the technology stolen from the Ptah Institute," he said. "But, much like the Romani here, many Bedouin tribes are known for clever clockwork creations. Saleh, a brilliant engineer, was one of the Ptah Institute's best and brightest. Who's to say what else he was working on when he stole his own creation and ran for Europe?"

"An oblique way of saying you'll have to look inside first?"

He grinned. "I can't deny looking forward to prying it open and inspecting the scarab's inner workings."

"So either Marston was directly targeted, or the clockwork creature works in a more random manner, visiting each supplicant to bestow a kiss and—" She frowned. "Relying upon chance for the poison to eliminate a specific person is... sloppy. Not at all how I would expect Harlowe to approach a situation."

An excellent point. "Unless he carefully preselected tonight's participants?"

"That's a grim thought," she said. "But would he categorize 'stark raving mad' as an acceptable outcome?"

"Or 'responsible for the death of another'?"

"He might." Their mutual acquaintance had a habit of stooping to low levels when he thought he could manipulate the outcome in his favor. He'd done it before. Graham inserted the master key into the slot of yet another tomb door. "Death presents a clean break. Witnesses are inconvenient."

Thunk. The bolt retracted.

Once again, the coffins were all cool to the touch, no sounds echoed inside the burial chamber and neither of them spied anything amiss. Not so much as a stray scrap of mummy wrappings or any other indications of past pseudo-pagan rites.

Graham shut the door and threw the bolt home. They moved on to the next tomb.

Again they found nothing. Again they moved on.

With rising impatience, they repeated the process over

and again with nothing breaking the morning silence save distant birdsong and the crunch of their footsteps on the gravel pathway. Tomb after tomb turned up nothing.

He huffed in frustration. "What if Marston didn't insist upon holding this unwrapping party inside, behind closed doors?"

"You think the gathering took place outside?" Julia paused, glanced over her shoulder. Behind them stretched acres of land studded with burial markers of all kinds. Her face dropped. "It's possible. Khepri does represent the rising sun." Her nose scrunched up and she shook her head. "No. Marston would value privacy and secrecy above all else."

Resigned, if not still doubtful, he turned the key in the seventh door of the seventh tomb. This time, the bolt retracted silently.

He glanced at Julia, eyebrows aloft.

"This one," she whispered in agreement, setting her basket carefully aside upon the ground. Ready to confront whatever they found within.

The door swung open upon well-oiled hinges. Not a creak or a groan echoed through the stone space.

Anticipation raced across his nerves. Was this *the* tomb? What awaited them? An abandoned mummy case? Evidence of a gathering gone horribly wrong?

He swept the light of his decilamp across the floor—suspiciously dust free—and the beam fell upon a yellowed scrap of aged linen.

"Discarded mummy wrappings?" Julia whispered beside him.

They stepped inside, pressing hands to coffins tucked into niches. All were cool to the touch. Except... He frowned, squinted at the ends of three coffins stacked above one another. Something about their alignment was strange, but the moment he lifted his decilamp to study the caskets, Julia gasped and tugged at his sleeve.

"Graham!" She slid the decilamp from his hand and directed the beam of light at the stone floor. "Look!"

"A stalk of Emmer wheat." Out of place, certainly, but it didn't account for the level of excitement in her voice. "What am I missing?"

Pinching her fingers about the stem, she rose. "Do you see the small, curved black structure that looks like an oversized grain of wheat gone bad?"

He squinted at the misshapen lump. Not at all appetizing. "From your excitement, I'm guessing it might belong to the mushroom family?"

"Not exactly." She turned the stalk from side to side, examining it as a whole. "While all mushrooms are fungi, not all fungi are mushrooms. This specimen falls into the latter category. Mushrooms are fruiting bodies, the reproductive part of a vast underground network of mycelium and, generally speaking, far larger. This is not a mushroom, but an ergot sclerotium, a compact mass of hardened fungal mycelium."

"Ergot," he repeated. Something about the word sounded familiar, but he was struggling to place it in context. Reclaiming the decilamp, he swept it across the floor once more. Coincidence would not drop both two out-of-place items—a stalk of wheat and a scrap of linen—directly before what he was beginning to think was a false wall.

"*Claviceps purpurea*. A fungus known to infest rye, wheat and barley. It's impervious to heat and, when baked into bread and ingested, the highly poisonous and psychoactive alkaloids—including lysergic acid—cause a condition known as ergotism. This was mostly only a major problem in the Middle Ages, though there was a recent outbreak in Germany."

"Symptoms?"

"Not priapism. Marston would have noted no change to his male member." Her lips twisted. "But the list is long. Seizures and muscle spasms. Headaches, nausea and vomiting. Mania and psychoses. The alkaloids can also cause blood vessels in distal regions—fingers and toes, hands and feet—to constrict leading to a condition known as dry gangrene. Entire limbs can sometimes be lost."

He cringed. "Hallucinations?"

"Most definitely." Academic enthusiasm meant she all but bounced on her toes, anchored to the floor only by the seriousness of the conversation. "Alternatively, it is sometimes called St. Anthony's Fire, named after a third century Egyptian ascetic who fought against horrible visions and temptations. A late medieval painter, Hieronymus Bosch, portrayed ergot hallucinations as scenes of frightening monsters and demons and other grotesque hellish images. All these bad bread experiences spawned the Order of St. Anthony, monks who set up hospitals, Europe's first specialized medical care system."

He twisted his lips, annoyed, but recalling relevant past events. "Bread. There was that dustup about Mummy Wheat not too long ago."

"Yes. Quite the hoax." Her voice vibrated with passion. "Someone claimed to have sprouted ancient grains recovered from linen wrappings but, when independent investigations examined grains beneath the lens of a microscope, the tissues were far too degraded to sprout. Wheat has a dormancy period of approximately twenty-five years. Two, three thousand years is far, far too long for the grain to have retained viability."

He struggled to understand her excitement. Bread was often offered to the Egyptian gods upon altars and was found in burials. It could not, however, be considered edible. Which wasn't to say someone hadn't baked a modern approximation.

"Not one person linked to the Order of the Winged Scarab has reported consuming bread, contaminated or otherwise."

She shook her head. "This is not about bread, it's about the clockwork scarab. Overwintered sclerotium will sprout to continue the lifecycle of the fungus, with each individual sclerotium forming up to sixty stromata."

"Stromata?" He recognized none of the scientific words she spouted.

"Tiny reproductive spore-producing structures with flesh-colored stalks about this long." She held up her finger and thumb to indicate a length a little less than an inch. "With small, spherical heads that could easily be mistaken as mushrooms." She held the stalk of wheat aloft. "*This* could be what I saw growing atop the carapace of the clockwork scarab."

"You believe the scarab is the source of these poisonous —" He stopped, forgetting the word, waiting for her to supply it.

"Poisonous alkaloids," she provided.

He flashed her a smile, pleased to be working with an expert who so readily offered an explanation that made all the pieces fall into place. "Those. In short, ergot poisoning." It connected their discovery to witnessed behaviors. "Temporary insanity with a chance of occasional death."

"The question is how the poison was administered." She tipped her head. "You mentioned a kiss."

"Oral consumption," he concluded. She was brilliant. Was it any wonder he'd lost his head over this woman? "We need to find that scarab."

"Our number one goal." Empty words that were the expected reply but were, in short, a lie. Locating the mechanical insect wasn't *his* immediate priority. Not when moments like this reminded him that all he wanted to do was drag her against his chest, wrap her in his arms and kiss her senseless. "We'll catch the scarab, then avail ourselves of your brilliant mycological insight."

Her eyes sparkled. "After which we'll pry it open and apply your engineering skills to analyzing its parts and pieces."

He tipped up her chin and parted her lips with a soft kiss. A small celebration to mark a step forward in their quest. A brief, stolen moment to bank until a more opportune moment.

Or so he promised himself. The tiniest of gasps escaped her throat, a sound that jolted alive a very specific memory.

The public galleries had been closed, the hour was late. But as an employee of the museum, he'd possessed a key. They'd slipped away to the empty, echoing Egyptian gallery to view a display of pottery fragments. His memories of the artifacts were vague, but he recalled every last sensory detail of their time behind a nearby statue. His palms braced against cool, hard sandstone as he sought out the sweet, honeyed depths of her mouth. The crush of her soft breasts against his chest as her impatient hands tugged and pulled the fastenings at his waistband. Buttons. Hooks. Ties. All undone that they might—

Julia pushed hard against his chest. Her head snapped back, eyes wide. "What was that?"

"What was what?" He struggled to calm his breathing, to slow the rushing of blood through his ears, that he might listen closely.

"A moan."

The only one he recalled was hers.

She pivoted to face the false wall— Ah, right. He'd yet to tell her about that because she'd found a black grain of wheat. Ergot.

His hands fell from her waist. "These coffins appear to conceal—"

"Listen!" she hissed, pressing a fingertip to his lips.

This time, he heard it. A low moan and a soft scratching.

"It's a façade. Look." He pointed with the decilamp. "Someone affixed the sawed-off ends of coffins to a wall, if sloppily. You can see the faint outlines of a door."

She bent forward tracing a fingertip along the gaps, her mouth open. "A disguised door, fashioned to keep people from finding some kind of hidden space." Her voice dropped to a horrified whisper. "Marston locked someone inside this tomb and left them to die?"

"It appears so. Purposefully? Hard to say, what with him under the influence of a drug. I certainly hope it wasn't intentional." The Egyptians had rarely practiced sacrifice, and that had died out with the First Dynasty some five thousand years ago.

All the blood drained from her face. "If we hadn't come looking..."

"We need to find the release mechanism."

He ran the light around the edges of the door's façade, hoping for a metallic glint that would reveal hidden hinges or a latch. Julia shoved at the lacquered wood coffin ends, searching for a concealed trigger.

This close to the panel, he could make out a faint whimper.

"Something shifted," she announced from a position that had her all but kneeling on the floor.

He dropped to his knees beside her, and together they pushed. Beneath their hands, wood groaned with only the slightest give.

"That brass coffin handle there." She pointed. "It's more

polished than it ought to be given the burial date engraved on the plaque. Try giving it a twist?"

With a firm grip, he wrenched the brass handle. There was a snap, a click and a pop. A section of the wall—the door —fell backward. A faint light glowed around its edges. "Brilliant, as always."

"Is someone there?" a high-pitched voice called. Female. "Help!" Her cries were accompanied by the sound of fingernails clawing at wood.

"Hang on!" Julia yelled back. "We're coming."

But the door opened no further. "Perhaps it slides sideways?"

Together, they gripped brass handles of false coffin ends and pulled. With a cacophony of screeching and groaning, the panel door slid sideways.

The scene before them was proof positive that this was where the Order of the Winged Scarab had held its most recent—and fatal—meeting.

Simple terracotta oil lamps flickered from ledges in the four corners of the room lending an air of mystery. Their flames flickered and wavered, the light guttering as the last of the oil burned.

In the center, a table held a mummy case, a coffin that was decidedly out of place inside an English burial chamber. The painted lid had been lifted away and propped against the far wall, exposing its partially unwrapped occupant.

Lengths of ancient linen lay in shreds upon the floor. Tiny amulets rested in piles upon the table beside a ceremonial dagger and an authentic—and likely plundered—

papyrus scroll that had been unrolled to a scene depicting the "opening of the mouth ceremony". How appropriate, then, that beside it stood a bottle and five empty wine glasses. Most damning, however, was the stone bowl that held a number of black grains. Ergot sclerotium. Plucked from the wheat frond they'd discovered?

Sprawled across the floor were two men and two women. The men were dressed in striped head cloths, linen kilts and golden sandals. The women adhered to current Parisian fashions, though rich embroidery and dense decorative beading introduced numerous Egyptian motifs in styles that —well, styles that had never existed. Ever.

All wore an overabundance of Egyptian jewelry, including wide pectorals featuring scarabs greeting the rising sun with wings outstretched.

The woman who had called for help clung to consciousness with a tenuous grip, and Julia fell to her knees beside her, shaking her shoulder and asking for her name.

Which freed Graham to hastily search the hidden chamber, the mummy case and the—he cringed—the mummy itself. But missing from the chaotic, absurd scene no matter where he looked? Technology.

The inquisitor wasn't here. But if not in Marston's possession last night, where was it? Or, rather, where had Harlowe stashed it?

It would have to wait. Time to examine the casualties of Harlowe's undertaking.

He drew a deep breath, cursed the man's name, then set about checking on the fallen supplicants.

Two individuals lay side by side: the wayward lordling and his bride, as recognized from the photograph Lady Tramontin had pressed into his hands. They still lived and breathed. Alas, there would be no assessing their mental state until they regained consciousness.

The second—unknown—gentleman was, however, the latest to be interned in Highgate Cemetery, however temporarily. Marston didn't count, Graham decided, expiring among the undergrowth as he had in an attempt to —escape? Find help? Either way, both would share morgue space before reaching their final resting places. Which meant all hopes of learning anything about the recent cere-mony depended upon their one conscious witness, now slumped against the stone wall.

He returned to them, crouching beside Julia who was waving an ostrich feather fan in front of the woman's face. "How is our victim?" A lady, judging from the gemstones studding her bodice and the heavy satin of her gown.

"She's complaining about the desert heat," she answered.

"Have you learned anything from her?"

"*Shabtis.*" The woman's voice was a strangled wail. "We are nothing but *shabtis.*"

Julia's lips twisted. "She keeps repeating a barely coherent narrative about how Khepri locked them all inside to serve as *shabtis.*"

"Funerary figures?" He frowned. "The ones meant to act as servants in the afterlife?"

"So I gather. Though they certainly aren't clay, wood or

stone. Nor are they tiny. But the hallucinations brought on by ergot poisoning may have convinced Marston otherwise."

"Locked us in," the woman moaned. "Not servants. Lords and ladies."

Wonderful. The deceased man at her side was likely in possession of a title, making the woman his widow. Information sure to set Black swearing a blue streak in Romani. Graham didn't envy the agent the task of informing next of kin.

He tipped the woman's face upward, flicking the decilamp across her eyes, then pressed two fingers to her wrist. "Dilated pupils. Rapid and weak pulse. Difficulty breathing."

"Consistent with ergot poisoning. She needs medical help. The others?"

"Two with pulses, one without." He patted the lady's face, gently at first, then harder, until she blinked and her eyes swam into focus. "What did you eat?"

"Black wheat," she said. "The men grew beaks and Lorraine turned inside out. We shrank. The beetle bit the professor and he caught on fire." Her head lolled from side to side. "Our mouths opened, but not one amulet worked, no matter how many spells we chanted."

Or, at least, that was what he made of her slurred words. "There's a fancy bowl with black grains of ergot on the table," he informed Julia.

"Sclerotium," she corrected, her mouth flattening into a line. "Wonderful. The party skipped right over the 'accidental ingestion in the form of bread' and moved straight to 'direct consumption'. A few sclerotia alone can prove fatal."

All while desecrating human remains and chanting inside a hidden burial chamber. Did it still qualify as a cult if the leader died during the initial ceremony?

He rose onto his feet. "Stay with her." Much as he hated leaving Julia behind—effectively alone—he suspected Harlowe would stay well clear of the cemetery for the time being. No point in ruining a good alibi by showing up at the crime scene. "I'll see if Jackson and the medics have arrived yet."

"See if they have any activated charcoal. Swallowing a few tablets might help. *Might*." She caught his arm. "The inquisitor?"

He shook his head. "Not here."

Outside the stone burial chamber, he blinked in the bright morning light. His feet crunched on the gravel as he ran toward a voice calling his name.

"Jackson!" he yelled. "Over here!"

Rounding the corner, he shot back onto the Egyptian Avenue. There, the other agent along with two men bearing a stretcher, not much more than two poles with a strip of canvas in-between to hold a patient, were headed his way. Catching sight of him, they picked up their pace.

"We collected Professor Marston," Jackson said. "Black sent us to check with you."

"Four more individuals," Graham reported. "Three with suspected ergot poisoning. One beyond any need of care. Do you have any activated charcoal?"

"In the ambulance," one answered. Then the three men disappeared into the open tomb. He was about to follow, to volunteer to carry the woman when a glint of sunlight caught his eye.

He paused beneath the sun disk-adorned stone lintel. And found himself staring into the eyes of a black clockwork canine for the second time in one day. Subtle differences marked this creature as unique. This one was broader across the chest. Knifelike teeth gleamed in its open jaws. A shaggy, wire coat bristled across its body. And there was no ignoring its hypnotic blazing red eyes.

"Gwyllgi," he breathed. A not-so-spectral clockwork Celtic hound stalked him in the broad daylight. One of the many black dogs that haunted Britain.

A shiver of insight made the fine hairs rise on the back of his neck and the air crackled with possibility. Such obvious and simple logic. How had he missed it?

Julia's voice broke the spell. "Graham?"

Dismissed by the medics, she stood by his side.

The mechanical hound turned and disappeared around the bend. There was no better proof that Harlowe was involved. He'd deliberately allowed Graham and Black to meet Anubis. Then sent the Celtic clockwork hound to collect the scarab instead.

He grabbed her hand and pulled, breaking into a run. "I know where to find the inquisitor."

CHAPTER NINE

Long skirts and a corset weren't the preferred attire for chasing clockwork creatures through a cemetery. Nor did carrying a basket containing precious mushrooms enhance her running speed. She might be out of breath, but there wasn't a mushroom's chance in the desert sun that she would stay behind and miss the grand capture.

If Julia had heard right, they were hot on the heels of a clockwork gwyllgi, the one Harlowe wanted to name Kynan, which was actively tracking—calling?—the clockwork scarab. The black wires that sprung from its back like long, stiff hairs glinted as the canine darted between and around gravestones —the only reason the mechanical animal wasn't traveling at full speed. If—when—it found the scarab, all hope of capturing Harlowe's minion would be lost.

"You... think... it has the... inquisitor?" Words exhaled between gasps of air. It wasn't that she doubted Graham or his instincts, but a loaf of bread and a black dog didn't bear much resemblance to each other in shape or size.

"I think it *is* the inquisitor!" he yelled back with little effort.

Julia knew a moment's envy for his ease of movement. But she couldn't place all blame on her clothing, not when she spent the vast majority of her days and nights pouring over books, pottery shards, and culture tubes. Of late, the most physical activity she'd engaged in was baking bread and small batch brewing of experimental ales and beer.

Behavior she needed to amend. A Queen's agent, or so she imagined, would need physical agility and cardiac endurance. She blushed, recalling their former intimate interpersonal bedroom activities. She definitely needed to build more activity into her day, so that she could keep up at night.

"Look!" he yelled, pointing without breaking his stride. A telescoping foot-long metal rod now protruded from the creature's back. "An antennae! It's calling the scarab!"

She jerked her head in acknowledgement, a nod of sorts, but was beyond managing a verbal reply.

Far ahead, at the other side of a stretch of green lawn, the canine had halted atop a broad stone slab of a gravestone. A rectangular section of the mechanical canine's back opened, exposing dark space within.

A receptacle for the scarab?

Graham released her hand, vaulted over a gravestone and increased his speed.

She slowed and paused a moment to brace her hand

against a tree and drag in great gulps of oxygen to calm her burning, protesting lungs. Then rejoined the chase.

A whirring, a buzz and a rustle of leaves announced the clockwork scarab's arrival moments before it burst out of a dense thicket in all its burnished copper and blue glory. Shimmering and glistening in the sunlight, the insect whizzed through the air, flying over Graham as both of them targeted the gwyllgi.

Graham was gaining on the clockwork canine and, for a moment, it looked as if he might catch them as the mushroom-studded beetle hovered over the clockwork dog's open back. Then, with a snap, the insect folded the thin, delicate vellum wings that held it aloft, snapping them beneath hard metal elytra, wing-cases, and dropped vertically.

He dove, arm outstretched, and wrapped his hand around the gwyllgi's metal ankle.

Snap. The hatch that had opened in the dog's back clicked into place.

Snap. The creature lunged at Graham's forearm with jagged, metal teeth. He shouted, releasing his grip, rolling away. But before he could regain his feet, the gwyllgi leapt from the gravestone and raced back onto the cemetery pathway.

"After it!" Graham yelled, resuming the chase.

Skirts gathered in her fist, Julia ran, basket banging against her hip as her boots dug into the gravel pathway.

Before them was an opening in the tall brick wall that ringed the cemetery. Nothing ornate, merely two tall, simple iron gates left ajar, a back entrance onto Swain's Lane. There was no hope of catching the clockwork hound again, not from the ever-growing distance that stretched between them.

The gwyllgi shot out onto the London street. Graham followed, hot on its heels.

There was a screeching and a clattering followed by the horrible sound of torn metal suggestive of an accident of drastic proportions.

Fear clutched her heart.

She burst through the gate and found Graham crouched, hands braced upon his knees. She fell backward upon the brick wall, lungs screaming.

Trompette de la Mort. He was safe.

All that effort and, while they'd not caught the clockwork canine, neither had it escaped them.

Scattered atop the cobblestones lay the remains of the clockwork dog. The gwyllgi had been pried open like a tin can, its innards removed. All that remained was scrap metal. A tubular torso. Legs with broken hinges and snapped pistons splayed at odd angles. Its tail tossed ten feet away like a discarded bottle brush. And yet—

"Where's... the head?"

Graham pointed.

Driving away at a rapid clip was an open barouche. A coachman upon a high box held the reins to a clockwork horse. Sitting inside was a woman wearing a red-striped skirt and a green vest over a white blouse. A colorful embroidered belt encircled her waist and she wore the oddest of hats, an unfashionable style almost never seen upon the streets of London.

Crownlike, red-felted and heavily beaded, an observer in the know—like Julia—would identify her headpiece as a traditional Latvian *vainag* worn by unmarried women. Breaking with tradition, additional material billowed and poofed above the crownlike base, not unlike that of a chef's hat, but in this case meant to resemble that of a mushroom. The pattern embroidered upon the circlet was a repeating *zvaigzne*, a star, representing the harmony of life and death.

Where did mushrooms grow?

Upon the dead and decaying.

The woman's eyes locked with hers and the slightest hint of surprise, then annoyance, flashed across the woman's countenance. As the barouche disappeared in the distance, she lifted a finger and pointed it—as if in accusation—at Julia.

"You know her?" The sound of Graham's voice brought her back into the moment. He'd darted out into the street and returned with the gwyllgi's remains.

"Know is a strong word." Julia swallowed. Did anyone ever know a *mathe*? "She goes by the name of Tatjana Skride. Is it her true name?" She shrugged. "Possibly. It is how I will introduce you."

He slanted her a curious glance. "Ought I be asking *what* she is?"

"She's Sēņu māte, of Latvian mythology. A goddess."

"Sēņu māte?" His eyebrows rose. "And that's Latvian for—?"

"Mother of Mushrooms." She'd never mentioned the woman or her shop to anyone outside her family. After all, an acquaintance with women purported to be Slavic goddesses would draw nothing but odd looks questioning one's sanity. She directed her gaze to the bent and misshapen clockwork creature at their feet. "You may find your inquisitor inside the hound's torso, but the scarab will be missing."

He crouched. Shook his decilamp to life, lifted a flap on what had been the gwyllgi's back and scanned the compartment. "Empty." Lips twisted, Graham examined the inner workings of the contraption and pulled forth a tangle of wires connected to paper-wrapped cylinders and flat button-like structures. "This, I think, may be the inquisitor, but I'll have to have our engineers at the Rankine Institute take a look to be certain." He lifted his eyes to focus upon her. "Now tell me about this mother of mushrooms who has possession of foreign technology we need to repossess."

Julia hesitated. Was it that she was unable or unwilling to accept what folklore put forth as fact? Partly. But it was also hard to dismiss this moment as mere coincidence. Sēņu māte had *known*.

"Julia?"

"She owns a shop with her sisters where all manner of culinary and medicinal plants and herbs—and, yes, mushrooms—are sold."

"And sometimes rides about in an open carriage, chasing down clockwork creatures?" Incredulous amusement tinged his voice.

"Chasing after mushrooms," she corrected.

Why? That remained to be seen.

"We'll need to visit her store as soon as we turn these scraps over to Jackson." He handed her the hound's tail, then tucked the rest of the contraption under his arm and turned back toward the cemetery gate. "This woman is involved somehow," he grumbled, "else how would she have known where to find the clockwork scarab?"

He was right, of course. Only not in the manner he believed.

She could explain, but he would think her mad. Better to let Graham form his own conclusions. "I'll take you to her," she said. "But first we need to make a brief stop."

He would object. And he wouldn't be wrong. But the mummy's body had already been desecrated. Easier than robbing another grave.

One did not approach goddesses without appropriate gifts in hand.

—>—❖—<—

"You stole a mummy's finger?" A rhetorical question given he was staring down at the blackened, shrunken skin that surrounded three phalanges. At an overgrown fingernail. At the wrinkles and folds that marked the bend of ancient knuckles.

"Animal bones don't suffice. It has to be human." Julia wrapped the digit in a scrap of linen torn from the hem of her petticoat and tucked it into her collection basket. "Many to choose from, one supposes, in a cemetery. But none quite so conveniently at hand."

The crank carriage they'd flagged down clicked and clattered as it sped back toward central London.

They'd returned to the tomb with the hidden annex and surrendered the pieces of the clockwork gwyllgi to Jackson, informing him of the chase, of the street collision. The agent nodded and waved them on, promising to send a message informing Black of this new development when he arrived at the Lister Institute. The bodies were already en route to the morgue and the medics were in the process of loading the last survivor onto a stretcher. They too would be transported to Lister, to the hospital wing where they would receive the best of care and be under supervision of the Queen's agents. Interrogations would begin once—if—they regained consciousness.

With that, he and Julia had exited Highgate Cemetery and sought out swift transportation.

"Human," he repeated. His mind struggled to fashion her words into a cohesive thought. And failed. She was no grave robber, no black-market dealer, no occult enthusiast. Facts which kept him from stopping the carriage and turning back. Well, that and the confidence she projected. She *knew* who had the clockwork scarab. Or so she claimed.

"I'm afraid so."

He ran his hand through his hair. Shook his head. "You're not making any sense."

She sighed. "I find it as revolting as you, but if we're to retrieve the scarab, there's little choice. Sacrifices must be made. The women who operate the store are Slavic goddesses and—"

"Are?" He shook his head. "You're not making sense. Gods and goddesses are human constructs—"

She pressed a finger to his lips. "Whether they are or aren't is immaterial. *They* believe and therefore we must act accordingly. We play by their rules and the scarab will be in our hands in a matter of minutes. Attempt to impose legal authority, and they're likely to melt away into the populace, taking the clockwork beetle with them."

He frowned, not quite able to accept her reasoning.

"Egypt and Britain will demand an explanation as to how the scarab escaped yet again. And the longer Harlowe walks free, the more time he has for damage control. Better he is caught off guard, forced to react without time to plot his course. He might well escape."

Her points were valid.

Still, he ought to decline, to insist that human remains not be handled as objects with bartering power. But he wanted that clockwork creature in his possession. A single ancient finger in exchange? Countless lives might be saved.

Setting the basket at her feet, she shifted upon the lumpy seat. Close enough that her thigh pressed against his. "Please?"

Her upturned face invited him to set aside his morals on several fronts. Their carriage was private. A chance for an affectionate exchange of a more physical nature.

"Fine." Her finger lifted from his mouth, slipped downward over his chin and hooked about his collar. Her honeyed breath drifted across his cheek. "I'll accept your plan as better judgment for the time being, but when we arrive at their store, if I think—"

She tugged, bringing his lips to hers. There was no more thinking, only instinct. Hunger gripped him. And a needy emotion that he couldn't pin down, one defined by an emptiness that only she could fill.

He'd expected a soft kiss, one that spoke of gratitude. But this was hot and demanding in a way that reminded him of the privacy carriages provided, of a better way to pass the minutes alone. He parted her lips and took the kiss deeper. Her arms locked around his neck as she fell backward against the worn fabric of the seat cushion. Together they toppled into a tangle of limbs.

She squirmed. "A spring beneath my back is broken."

He slid an arm beneath her, cushioning her against the lumps and hard jabs of the much-abused seat. "Better?"

"Much."

"Where were we?" He jammed a foot against the carriage wall, dismissing the way it bowed outward. It held. That was all that was required.

His mouth fell at her throat, at the swell of her breast. He yanked at the fabric of her bodice, smiling against her skin when her corset offered up a hard nipple surrounded by the enticing pink of her areola.

"Graham." Her voice was a whisper as she threaded her fingers into his hair and drew his head close.

Greedy, he pulled its entirety into his mouth and was rewarded by a cry that sent lust exploding through his veins. He circled her nipple until she was squirming and thrusting her hips against him. Against his hard member that begged for release.

His hand slid lower, grabbed the soft folds of fabric below her knee and hauled them upward. Free from the tangle of skirts, her shapely legs wrapped in plain stockings were a tantalizing vision. Especially where they ended and the frilly lace of her drawers began.

His hand tightened on the fabric as she shifted, parting her legs. Both encouragement and invitation to explore.

But if he allowed himself this indulgence, they wouldn't stop.

They never had.

No matter the location.

Even now, her hands were at his waistband, expertly freeing one brass button after the next. Soon her soft fingers would wrap around him, stroke him in a manner that would drive him mad enough to toss aside the last fraying shreds of his manners, to free himself and plunge into her soft, welcoming wetness to finally—*finally*—satisfy them both.

His bones were melting as his blood turned to liquid fire. All while his heart slammed up against his chest wall and every primitive instinct insisted upon the immediate fulfillment of its carnal cravings.

But his frontal cortex disagreed.

The coiled spring beneath his wrist stabbed and grit grinding beneath the sole of his shoe were a reminder that this was a place for a quick romp, not one for a memorable reunion. Not with the woman he hoped to make his wife.

He could wait a few hours. Even a few days.

Willing blood to flow again to his frontal cortex, he forced physical desire back inside its cage and locked the door. It growled and hissed, but the bars held burning need at bay with promises of "soon".

"Julia," he breathed. A final adoration whispered across soft bare skin before he pulled away. "Much as I want you, want this." He dragged in a deep breath as she tugged her bodice back into place, as he refastened buttons. "We should stop."

"Not the setting you had in mind?" The corners of her mouth curved up.

"Not even close. I want to be able to see you. All of you." The light that managed to elbow its way past the window's accumulated grit and grime was meager and not at all conducive to a romantic mood. "And if the carriage is stopped, for any reason..."

"You're right, of course." She sighed. "We ought to converse. How is your family? Tell me about your life as an engineer and a spy? But the next time we're alone behind a locked door..."

He grabbed her chin and gave her one last soul-searching kiss.

"They're fine, enjoying the country life of a squire, a commissioned officer and a vicar."

"So very traditional." She smiled. "You remain the sole rebel."

"If they only knew. Digging about in the dirt and shooting ionizing rays at pottery is bad enough." He grinned. "About that."

He sat back and began a story. One with a purpose. He'd not returned with a ring—or any jewelry for that matter—believing an intimate future with her beyond his wildest hopes and dreams. As it was, this moment felt ephemeral, as if it might be snatched away in an instant. A reminder that his gift suffered and was in need of her expert care.

The gift he'd carefully carried across multiple borders was something she'd spoken of with longing since the day they'd first met.

Yeast.

But not just any yeast.

"A group of archaeologists to our north located a predynastic site with evidence of beer production."

Her eyes widened. "Go on."

"They found a large, semi-buried vat with thick fire-resistant walls—"

"Wort vessels?"

Boiling wort was an important step that improved clarity and drove off unwanted volatile compounds. But even more importantly, it killed off bacteria and encouraged yeast growth.

He nodded. "One large enough to hold eighty gallons. Inside it was what looked like residues of—"

"Caramelized sugars? Grain debris?" Her excitement rose with each word.

He nodded. "Nearby were other vessels."

"Fermentation jars?" She pressed her hands to her chest when he nodded, enthralled. "When they return from their excavation, will you introduce me?"

He knew of her planned experiments. She'd spoken of them often enough. And he'd listened. Carefully. All she needed was an ancient beer jug, a piece of pottery thousands of years old that had lay buried in the sand, undisturbed. Then, she would perform yeast collection.

Not that you could merely scrape the surface. No, that would result only in a contaminated sample, given its external contact with any number of things. Instead, using a sterile syringe and a cotton ball, he'd carefully infused the clay matrix with a nutrient bath. Then you waited. Waited for any long-dormant organisms to wake up and sense the new, suddenly favorable environment around them. Then, using that same syringe, he'd vacuumed the liquid back out and transferred it to a flask.

That had been the easy part. Keeping the ancient yeast alive was proving far, far more difficult.

He reached inside his coat. "I'll do better than that, I'll—"

The crank hack skidded and slid on its worn wooden wheels as it came to a sudden and screeching halt. His eyebrows slammed together as his grin fell away.

Were they always destined to be interrupted, to never have enough time to—

Julia already had her basket in her lap and was pulling on a pair of gloves when a fist rapped at the door. "We're here!"

"Here?" he asked, frowning. "I thought we were headed to Whitefriars?"

"We are. I asked the driver to make a quick stop." She

pressed a leather-clad palm to his knee. "There's more than one goddess to appease. A few minutes only."

She all but leapt from the carriage, weaving through a thin crowd and making her way into a florist shop. Perhaps she meant to arrive with a bouquet?

He slumped against the seat and dropped his head back, blew out a long, frustrated breath and stared at the horse-hair stuffing that protruded from a rip in the rough canvas. He ought to be grateful. Flowers were much better than human remains.

CHAPTER TEN

Julia straightened her bodice and smoothed her skirts, summoning every last ounce of patience. Rushing through an encounter with goddesses was ill-advised, no matter how badly she wished to return to the pub. Where doors locked and privacy could be assured.

When she thought of approaching Sēņu māte, of petitioning her help, her heart jumped and skittered. Only once had she visited their place of trade. And that had been in the company of her own mother whose Latvian heritage was embedded in her very being, as part and parcel of her life. This time, she was on her own. She drew a deep breath and held it, steadying her breath and slowing her racing heart, reminding herself of the time-honored traditions and would not stumble.

Graham tossed the driver a coin and promised him extra if he waited. With one arm, he held the potted pine tree—wrapped in green tissue paper and tied with a bow—while helping her down from the crank hack at the end of a shadowed alleyway. Close-spaced buildings with crooked overhangs prevented even the noontime sun overhead from reaching the cobblestones beneath their feet. At number nine, a vine sprouted from the ground, claiming space by forcing aside a rock. How the plant managed to grow in such poor soil, to reach skyward, to branch and stretch until it formed a canopy arching over the entryway defied explanation.

A bit of wild inside the city refusing to cede ground to human interference.

Beneath the vine, she stopped before a plain brown door with a brass knocker. Carved into the wood just above the handle was a symbol, a square divided into quarters, but tipped onto its point such that it resembled a diamond. From the center of each side jutted a short line that branched into two outward curves.

Graham surveyed the darkened brick, the dim windows. The lack of a sign clearly identifying what was sold within.

"The perfect place for witches," he quipped, his disapproval evident.

"You're not wrong." She slid the handle of the basket to the crook of her arm, wishing she'd dared leave it in another's care.

He frowned. "You recognize the symbol?"

"It's a Slavonic talismanic solar motif," she said. "One said to represent the chicken-legged house of Baba Yaga."

"Baba Yaga," he repeated, eyebrows lifted. "The Russian witch?"

Julia lifted a shoulder. "Witch. Wise woman. Healer. Earth goddess. Forest grandmother. Many names have been given to her. If you must address her, 'Grandmother' is safest."

"Safest?"

As she reached for the door handle, Graham shifted, ready to step in front of her. He slid his hand beneath his jacket to rest upon his weapon, not at all trusting what they would encounter within.

"Don't." She paused before entering. "They won't hurt me." Not directly or overtly, in any case. "I'm the petitioner, not you. I enter first, else we'll be given no answers."

"I don't like this." Words that emerged as an objection, not an agreement to her request.

What they liked didn't matter. Not that she was afraid, but cautious. Bedtimes filled with stories of old Slavic gods and goddesses had taught her respect was paramount. And to be wary and arrive with gifts. Ones that carried a note of sacrifice. She pursed her lips, not wanting to argue, but prepared to do exactly that. There would be no conceding this point. "Do you want the scarab or not?"

Tight-lipped, he stepped back.

She pulled open the door.

A bell rang overhead, alerting the sisters as they stepped onto the creaky wooden floor of the store. No modern gas lights burned within, no Lucifer lamp rocked to cast a blue-white glow. Instead, candles placed on various surfaces burned, some of them threatening the dried bundles of herbs that hung from twine overhead. Wide-mouthed glass jars held all manner of dehydrated objects, including an assortment of mushrooms and roots. Some of them were culinary. Most, however, were not. Books and bottles of all shapes and sizes cluttered the shelves that lined the rooms, the contents of both unknowable, written as their titles and labels were in the Slavic languages. Spices and seasonings. Rinds and peels. Potions and remedies. Tinctures and tonics.

Unwise to help oneself.

An old woman with a large beaked nose and long, unruly gray hair barely contained by the flowered scarf tied beneath her chin stood behind a counter, using a mortar and pestle to grind an unidentifiable herb with great vigor.

She glanced up with narrowed eyes, seemingly annoyed at the appearance of customers. Not that she took any notice of Graham, for her beady eyes focused upon Julia, her expression one of barely contained disgust. "You."

Julia stepped forward, recognizing she treaded on thin ice, and held out her linen-wrapped offering. "For you, Grandmother. Ancient and from a distant land."

With suspicion in her gaze, the old woman snatched it from Julia's hands, quickly untying the knotted fabric and exposing—

"A mummy's finger?" Baba Yaga tipped the gift from side to side, examining it from all angles. Satisfied with its appearance, yet still suspicious, she raised the dried skin and bone to her nose and inhaled deeply, holding the scent inside her lungs. "Real," she pronounced, "and only recently unwrapped. It will serve as seasoning for Sunday's soup."

Beside her, Graham drew breath to protest. Convincing

him to exchange the ancient remains for access to the mother of mushrooms had not been easy. Learning that the mummy's flesh and bone were to be destroyed, to be consumed as a special treat might bring negotiations to an end.

Julia jabbed a sharp elbow into his ribs and gave a shake of her head. His jaw tightened, but he stayed silent.

Baba Yaga's gaze darted to Graham, then slid back to Julia, considering. "An acceptable apology, if meager."

Julia exhaled. They'd passed the first test.

"But you still have much to answer for, young lady." With a huff, the wise woman abandoned her work and turned to exit through an arched doorway, calling, "Sister! She's here."

Julia snatched the potted pine from his arms and pushed her collection basket into his hands. "Hold this." The next gift also needed to come from her.

"Black will skin me alive if—when—he learns of that exchange," Graham grumbled under his breath as they stood in the center of the store, awaiting the audience with Sēṇu māte. "This had better work."

She liked it no more than him. That's why it was considered a sacrifice. "It will."

He huffed, unconvinced. "Care to explain her cannibalistic tendencies?"

"In the old country, Baba Yaga is said to kidnap children to roast. To live in a chicken-legged house surrounded by a fence of human skulls and bones. The cemetery with a unique specimen was nearby." Unusual age, she hoped, would compensate for... newly harvested. "I improvised. Now hush."

The woman from the barouche, Tatjana Skride, stepped into the store looking no older—or younger—than she had since Julia had first met her. Fifteen years ago.

Mother had all but fainted when the goddess first set foot in the pub, leading her to a central table and serving her wild mushroom and potato soup alongside thick slices of rye bread made with the sourdough starter she'd carried with her from Latvia. In turn the goddess had blessed their tavern with good fortune. Which had endured for the entirety of her mother's life.

After which Sēņu māte had not returned. A bad omen.

The goddess crossed her arms and jutted her chin. "Did you think I wouldn't feel it moving?"

Beside her, Graham shifted. "Feel what, exactly?"

"We were doing our best to stop it," Julia answered. The mother of mushrooms wasn't referencing the clockwork scarab. Not exactly.

"Fungi are not meant to move about on legs," Sēņu māte replied. "Why were they brought into London?"

"Profit," she answered, setting aside the mother's use of the plural for later consideration. It meant something, but she needed to focus on the current conversational thread. Why? Harlowe certainly coveted money, but that wasn't all he was after. She added, "Power."

"Murder," Graham added. "All planned in advance by a sly man."

The mother's eyes narrowed. "He *intended* harm?"

Julia pressed her lips together and gave a tight nod. It hurt to admit so. He'd been a sharp annoying pebble in her shoe these past months, courting her attention and putting Marston in a cross mood. She'd thought him underhanded, but not actively malicious. A vast misjudgment, given the mounting evidence.

"He did," Graham confirmed. "Two people on British soil are dead. The clockwork creature's handlers left a swath of damage and death across Europe as they traveled. We need the device to bring them to justice."

Sēṇu māte waved a dismissive hand. "The technology is of no concern now that it has been stopped."

He drew breath to argue, but the goddess arched an eyebrow and he thought better of his objection.

She returned her focus to Julia. "What have you to say for *your* sins?"

Graham would think her mad, but she needed to issue a formal apology. "I broke the circle of mushrooms," she confessed. "Unintentionally. Shocked by the discovery of my husband's body, I lost awareness of my surroundings and landed inside the fairy ring.

"I took no more than the circle could bear," Julia defended herself. She held out the paper-wrapped potted tree. Much as it pained her to part with one of the few specimens she'd collected, the mother of mushrooms must be appeased, not angered. "I'm certain *Tricholoma* will flourish under your care. Any cultivation techniques you might be willing to share would be welcome."

Sēṇu māte tugged at the ribbon and let the paper fall

away to reveal a four-inch-tall pine sapling. Tucked beneath its needles in rich, dark soil was the fruiting body of a single, gently glowing matsutake mushroom. For a long moment, she examined its soft glow. Or such would be her actions as observed by someone with no knowledge of forest divinities.

Julia wasn't so certain the mother's study was purely visual. Did she speak to it? Merely listen? Something more? Sēņu māte, human-appearing as she was, could pull on her connections with all mushrooms, all fungus, all yeast in the London environs as if she and they were all connected by some giant underground mycorrhizae.

Quietly, Sēņu māte set the gift upon the counter. "It's lovely. And unique." She fixed Julia, then Graham, with a stern gaze. "Now to my concerns. Ergot fungus, wandering free, is an anathema. All summer, I felt its approach. Crossing distant soil, drawing ever closer. In my care, it roams free no more. What assurances do I have that it will not be set free again?"

"The Egyptians merely want their technology returned," Graham said. "We've caught the man who initiated the trouble. He's in custody. Unfortunately, he sold it to our target, to the man who used it to deliver death to two people last night. Put simply, he extracted wealth from noblemen and women with promises of a transformative experience."

"Hallucinations that can lead to death," the mother said.

Graham nodded. "Once we've proven the malice behind his actions, he will be brought to justice. The ergot will be destroyed, the mechanical parts returned to their creators."

An answer that seemed to satisfy the mother of mushrooms. "And what offering do *you* bring me?" Her gaze fell upon Julia's collection basket.

"For the mechanical creatures?" Graham blinked, momentarily confused. "No." He returned the basket to Julia, shook his head. "This is not mine to give."

Julia mentally chided herself. She'd thought only of the indiscretions of which she would be accused, never thinking that gifts would be expected of Graham as well. With promises of beer, bread and Jāņu siers, midsummer cheese, upon her lips, she opened her mouth. "Sēņu māte, I will—"

The mother held up a finger. "It is his request *and* he has an appropriate gift of his own."

His hand fell atop his chest and sucked in a breath. "It's not—"

"For me," the goddess finished. "But for your love. I'm aware. Yet it struggles in the environment you've created. Too long it was forgotten beneath the sand." She beckoned with her fingers. "Hand it over. I will save it."

"Save what?" Julia asked, turning to Graham. "What is she talking about?"

"This." He tugged the lapel of his coat aside and unbuttoned an inner flap. From a hidden pocket, he pulled out a corked test tube. Inside a thick brownish-yellow substance swirled.

Her eyebrows drew together. "Is that a starter culture?" If so, the mother of mushrooms was correct, it did not bubble enough. "Why do you—"

"I carried it with me from Egypt." Graham's gaze locked with hers. "I gained permission to collect this sample and have all the official documents. I managed to extract the yeast using the nutrient broth you've detailed—yes, under sterile conditions, a considerable feat in an archeological camp—from one of the ancient beer jugs."

"For me?" Flowers and poems and precious stones could not compare. No better gift existed. Moreover, he'd arranged to do so knowing she was unattainable, that there was no future for them—at the time—beyond a tenuous platonic relationship.

"For you. As a peace offering." He slid a look toward Sēņu māte. "For her studies. For her brewing efforts."

Such were his words, but Julia read more in the disappointment that filled his eyes. This yeast culture was a labor of love. One he could safely gift to a married woman.

The thought and effort that had gone into his present touched her soul.

The mother of mushrooms sighed. "It barely lives." She crooked her fingers. "Pass it here. It's not at all a fair exchange for the ergot, but this one time I'll overlook the discrepancy."

He hesitated.

Julia winced. But to save her pub, to collect the evidence against Harlowe, she must bite her tongue. A sacrifice was, was it not, what gods and goddesses demanded?

"Julija, tell him what he must do." Sēņu māte grew impatient, her voice revealing an accent.

No one had pronounced her name such since her mother had died. Any Lithuanian spoken among her and her sisters had gradually faded to a phrase or two scattered among casual conversation. Until now, she'd not realized how much she'd missed the sounds of her mother's homeland. Neither she nor her sisters had made much effort to preserve this part of their heritage.

A tear slipped from the corner of her eye and she dashed it away. Why did it always fall to her to set aside her hopes and dreams?

There was no choice. The small gift of yeast would prevent Mr. Black from meeting Baba Yaga. Better for all considered that the Crown require no deities to explain themselves.

"Let her have it." Julia whispered the response on a resigned breath of air. Two *Tricholoma* mushrooms remained in her collection basket. They were prize enough for today.

Graham frowned and the mother snatched the test tube from his hands, nodding her approval. "Come."

CHAPTER ELEVEN

Graham didn't care at all for Julia's meekness inside this store, in the presence of these supposed goddesses. Not one bit. Where was the woman who pushed and challenged and guarded her pub and research with a sharp tongue and stubborn will?

This mother of mushrooms couldn't be a real goddess with actual powers. That was impossible. Though her knowledge of the location of fungi within London's—England's, Europe's—borders was disconcerting at best. There was, no doubt, an explanation. If one he couldn't quite grasp.

Still, he would honor Julia's wishes—dare he say belief?—and tread with caution.

The woman led them into a back workroom. The shop was cluttered and mysterious but organized. This hidden space was a riot of chaos. Nothing was labeled. Mortars and pestles had been abandoned mid-use and a peppery aroma filled the humid air. There was a steady drip, drip, drip as flasks collected liquid from distillery apparatuses. On the countertops, pile upon pile of plants and roots and mushrooms threatened to tip over and cascade onto the floor. A large hanging cauldron bubbled over a wood fire inside an enormous fireplace. It was as if he'd stepped one hundred years into the past.

Sēṇu māte collected a flask, flour, and water, ignoring more exotic options. He frowned, failing to see how the yeast he'd collected in Egypt would thrive any better under her care as he'd used exactly the same ingredients.

"It's an understandable mistake, but this yeast needs distilled water and *emmer* wheat," the woman answered, as if reading his mind. She tipped a measure of flour into the flask, then added water, stirring the mixture before yanking the cork from his test tube and dumping the contents into her superior concoction. "There." She inhaled deeply. "Much better."

She yanked a white cloth from the counter and dropped it over the mouth of the flask. "So it may breathe."

Fine. She'd rescued the ancient yeast. But to what end? So it could bubble and froth on a dusty shelf behind fistfuls of dried leaves?

"The scarab?" He almost barked the words, impatient as he was to exit this odd store, to return to the more familiar ground of The Monocled Raven.

Lips pressed into a thin line at his near-disrespect, Sēṇu māte tossed aside a tea towel, revealing the clockwork scarab.

"Oh, Mother," Julia sighed. "What have you done?"

A small pair of traction tweezers had been inserted in the creature's throat—if a clockwork beetle could be said to possess one—prying it open. An optic magnifying tube had been inserted.

"How was I to know its purpose without looking inside at the internal mechanisms?" The woman tsked. "Easy enough to understand the creature's purpose, if somewhat more difficult to comprehend how it functions." She frowned. "Though the function of these gadgets and gizmos are much beyond me, it's easy enough to draw conclusions." She waved a hand, inviting them to perform their own inspection.

Julia picked up a magnifying glass and bent over the mechanical scarab. "Its carapace is covered with tiny white mushrooms, all of them protruding from tiny holes drilled through the metal. *Mycena stylobates*, the bulbous bonnet. Curious. But that cannot be what killed Marston or the others." Her eyebrows drew together, puzzling over their significance.

Sēṇu māte nodded her agreement. "A common enough mushroom in Europe. Inedible, if considered nonpoisonous."

Julia moved to peer down the optic magnifier. "Look!" She waved Graham forward. "Is that a—"

"Grinding mechanism?" He nodded. "It appears so. And a small belt with clockwork mechanisms was designed to convey the powder forward to the mouth parts."

"The kiss of the scarab," Julia said. "The purplish-black powder contained within the beetle's abdomen is ergot? You're certain, Mother?"

"You need to ask?" The woman pulled out the optic magnifier and tugged her traction tweezers free. "More than enough to poison a roomful of men and women." She lifted the clockwork scarab and pointed. "This is the 'off' switch. But to be safe—"

With little care, the mother of mushrooms popped the beetle into a small birdcage and secured its wire door. Graham cringed. The Ptah Institute would want all technology returned in working order and, given the shredded state of the clockwork gwyllgi, he hoped she'd done no permanent damage to the scarab with her tools.

Or, rather, to the tethersync inquisitor that worked in tandem with the magnetic orienter of the inquisitor, a miniaturized piece of technology that ought to be inside the artificial insect, carefully soldered within its thorax.

Sēṇu māte handed the cage to Julia and fixed her with a look. "Such mycological murder and mayhem cannot be allowed to continue. Don't let this fall into the wrong hands again. Be warned, however, these are not the only specimens in London that have been on the move."

"There are more?" he asked. "More clockwork insects?"

"More mushrooms," the woman corrected. "There were and may be again. As of this moment, however, they are sedentary. I will listen for them."

A mysterious comment. He chose not to ask for further explanation. Perhaps Julia understood.

Into his hands, Sēṇu māte shoved an old flour sack tied with twine. Beneath the cloth, he felt the hard outline of the disembodied gwyllgi's head. "If there's a next time, I'll stop by Clockwork Corridor and surrender it directly to the Roma." A threat as they'd disassemble the creature for parts and study long before any Queen's agents could locate them. Next, she held out the birdcage with a warning scowl. "It cannot be allowed to scurry about. If I need to chase this contraption down again, I will carry it directly to a smithy and see it melted into a puddle."

"Understood." He shot a resigned glance at the cloth covered flask. Julia had long fantasized about collecting an ancient yeast from an archeological dig, specifically one used in the process of brewing beer. He'd taken such care, so many pains, to collect and transport the tiny beasties. And had been on the verge of presenting his gift.

He suppressed a sigh. Work prioritized above love. Again. But if this is what Julia wanted, he would bite back his resentment and let the mushroom goddess keep it.

He was about to issue a final polite word of gratitude before insisting they needed to depart, except it seemed the Mother wasn't done handing out gifts.

"Julija." The woman decanted half the now-bubbling yeast mixture into a wide-necked bottle and snapped its cap closed. "You possess emmer wheat?"

"Of course." Hope bloomed on her face.

"Possibly einkorn would be acceptable, but no durum wheat," the woman said. "You might experiment with a touch of honey when you shape bread—but cane sugar will offend them."

Yeast with feelings?

But Julia didn't roll her eyes. Instead, she nodded.

What did she understand about the instructions that left him confused? Had he been chastised for not using ancient ingredients? Domesticated wheat had a long history, entire lineages that branched this way and that, so it must mean something even if the reasoning escaped him.

He would ask. Later.

With a few polite words and Julia's promise to bring the mother of mushrooms a sample of her first brewing of matsutake ale, they had nearly escaped, caged clockwork creature in hand, when the door flew open.

"Who brought the screaming rocks into our home?" The young, blonde woman's focus narrowed upon Graham.

Not again.

"Clarify, Žemyna." An even-toned request made by Sēņu māte.

Was this yet another presumed goddess? Julia *had* mentioned a trio of women.

"This man," the new woman pointed at his rucksack. "Possesses rocks that have been forcibly moved beyond singing and tortured until they screamed." She reached for the flap of his bag.

He took a step backward, in no mood to pacify another goddess with yet more gifts. "Step aside and we will remove them from your property."

Žemyna swept deeper into the store, waving him toward the door before pressing her hands on either side of her head. "Go. And hurry. My ears ring. They cry relentlessly for the creature's attention yet will be unsatisfied by its touch."

The door slammed behind them and they hurried down

the alleyway. Only returned to the relative safety of the crank hack did he ask, "What was that?"

"Who," Julia corrected. "An earth goddess."

He groaned.

"Mock if you must, but you suspected the pectorals called to the clockwork scarab from the beginning."

"Screaming rocks?"

"Magnetized stones emit a field of some sort, do they not?"

So they did.

CHAPTER TWELVE

Graham ran a hand through his hair, then shook his head, muttering about personifying inanimate objects.

Not wanting to dismiss Sēṇu māte's observations or the supernatural connections she might sense, Julia suggested a modern, scientific reinterpretation. "Magnetized stones emit an electromagnetic field, do they not? Perhaps she's sensitive to the alteration of materials mined from the Earth?"

Graham frowned. "I'm not at all comfortable admitting any of those women are deities or that they are in possession of anything resembling magical properties."

"Nor am I. And yet, they *knew*." She leaned forward, hand upon his arm. "They knew."

He sighed. "Wrapping wires around iron and connecting them to a power source such as a battery can induce a magnetic charge. I can't discount the possibility out of hand. We'll need to examine the jewelry much more closely."

Tension fell from her shoulders, lightening her heart. It meant a lot, his willingness to consider the possibility that the three sisters with a nameless store sensed that which they could not.

"My early ears were filled with all manner of superstitions from my mother's homeland," she said. "Mostly we just went along with what we perceived as Mother's 'silliness'. But those women? Before she died, Sēņu māte crossed the threshold of The Monocled Raven every August." She glanced down at the bubbling flask in her hands. "My mother would always serve her—free of charge—beer, bread and cheese. Nothing else, only products of fermentation. In return, or so my mother insisted, business flourished. After her death, my father barred the doors to Sēņu māte and, ever since, encountered nothing but setbacks with his business."

"There's no proving superstitions." An objection, but she knew his heart wasn't in the soft-spoken words. He doubted his own beliefs but wasn't quite ready to accept an alternative.

"And yet she knew." Her words softly spoken.

He grunted, neither agreeing nor disagreeing that the three women with inexplicable abilities might just possess abilities that most humans did not.

A comforting, yeasty scent wafted upward from the bubbling flask she held. There was no better way Graham could have demonstrated his enduring love.

How long had this yeast lain beneath desert sands, forgotten as time passed? Found, extracted from a fragment of pottery likely destined for a dusty box in a dark corner of a dusty museum basement. Rescued at the last minute by a gentleman whose heart held a tendril of affection for a woman who had turned him away, who had chosen another. Revived and tended, carried in a pocket against his chest across an entire sea, across an entire continent, making its way to a distant land.

"Thank you for this. It means... everything." She lifted the flask, marveling at how fast the yeast had sprung back to life. No starter culture could recover so quickly. Save, perhaps, one coddled and coaxed by the hands of Sēṇu māte.

She raised a hand to Graham's face, catching at his chin and pulling his lips to hers. Pouring her love and gratitude into a kiss, one that quickly heated and began to speak of need. Immediate need. His tongue parted her lips, and he dropped the cloth sack containing the gwyllgi's head to drag her closer. Desire threaded through her veins, twisting and spiraling until it stole her breath away.

She whimpered into his mouth, pleasure tinged with frustration. Late at night alone in her bed, she'd replayed memories of their time together, trying to reconcile herself to her circumstances, ones she herself had orchestrated. Not that she would have signed the marriage certificate if she'd known her family's pub would become a front for an antiquities dealership. Still she bore the responsibility for her current situation. Not for her husband's death, not directly. But if she'd gone to the authorities, agreed to Mr. Black's terms more readily...

That Graham was willing to give her a second chance meant everything.

And yet.

She'd never lived alone. Never controlled her future, not entirely. Now, widowed, her life was hers to control. Hers alone.

Provided, of course, they were able to catch Harlowe and pin this entire mess upon him.

His lips slid along the edge of her jaw, pressed a kiss behind her ear, then whispered the beginning of a question, "If the pub is empty…"

"Will I permit your continued physical attentions?" she finished. "No."

The hand running upward along the boning of her bodice hesitated.

"I'm rather inclined to demand them."

He laughed softly. "As you command, goddess." His thumb ran over the soft wool of her bodice, teasing her nipple with promises and setting free a cascade of long-denied desires.

Did she dream of a future with Graham? Yes. But not merely as his wife. The future held so many possibilities and a swift trip down the aisle wasn't one of them. What did her heart want? Graham. Her head valued academic acknowledgment and honors. But were her head and heart *both* agreed? They longed for a tavern to call her own. Hers. One where items on the menu were crafted from tradition, the more unusual and historical the better. Where word of mouth drew appreciative customers from all over London.

Not that she was limited to only one of those options.

The crank hack jerked to a stop, tearing them apart. Breathless, they stared at each other.

He turned his head, glancing out the grimy window to assess The Monocled Raven. "Agents standing guard."

She cursed. "Inside?"

"No." A hard kiss landed upon her lips, then he pushed her basket into her hands. A smokey heat filled Graham's eyes. "Head inside. I'll see to it that they don't follow."

"Please." A single word promising him—them—much should he succeed.

Motivated, he alighted with all due speed. He handed her down, paid the driver, gathered their spoils, and addressed the men who stood sentry at her pub's door. "Any sign of Harlowe?"

They shook their heads. "No word from Black, either." Answering as they stared at the caged scarab. "Is that—"

"It is." He lifted the flour sack as well, tipping his head to indicate its contents were of vast importance. "And then some. Mrs. Marston and I need to examine the recovered technology in some detail. We do not wish to be disturbed while we draw conclusions and plan our next steps. Let us know if—when—you apprehend Harlowe. Otherwise, please convey our update to Black." He tugged a slip of paper and a pencil from his pocket and began to scratch out a message.

Leaving them to their discussion, Julia unlocked the door and stepped inside the dark, deserted pub. In times past, the first customers would be scattered about, the beginnings of a crowd that would steadily grow—along with the noise—late into the night.

Would she be able to coax the return of old patrons, let alone draw in a new set? Would the government see fit to recognize her claim upon the property and not simply snatch away what should be rightfully hers? Much depended upon proving Harlowe's guilt. Did they possess enough evidence to convince a judge? How much could this Mr. Black influence outcomes? Could she continue living here, where bad memories swirled in the dark, dusty corners? Could she afford to start over elsewhere?

Questions best reserved for another day.

She shoved them aside.

Julia slid her hatpin free and tossed it and her hat upon a pub table. A few steps later, she dropped a glove upon the floor. Tossed the second over her shoulder as she passed the bar and rounded a corner, heading into the kitchens. There, she set the bubbling flask and her mushroom basket carefully upon the large wooden kitchen table.

Grabbing the terrarium she'd prepared that morning, she quickly dug holes in the loose soil, planting the pine sapling with the bioluminescent matsutake mushrooms tucked beneath its tiny branches. With care—and luck—they would form a symbiotic union and flourish.

She set the glass canister upon a shelf and froze. Turning slowly, she scanned the array of jugs, vases, bottles, pitchers and apothecary jars that ringed her kitchen. Had she a mushroom for a brain? Was it unwise setting up a fairy ring in her own home, even if the fungi that grew were of different species?

No. Fairy rings grew organically. She'd not accidentally

formed an enchanted circle. A thought she'd have dismissed as superstition a few hours ago, yet with the events of the day...

Still, she'd rearrange them later. Gather them together upon their own shelving unit. Shaking off the uncomfortable thought, she crossed the room to the sink.

With her hands washed, she dragged a stool across the room and climbed, reaching for the topmost shelf for her canister of emmer wheat. Shipped to her from distant Morocco at a steep price, she prayed the months of storage hadn't left it rancid. She pried open the lid and sniffed. A relief. Still good.

Back at the table, her hands flew down the buttons of her bodice. She shrugged it free, pulled off her corset cover and reached for an apron. Beer took too long and, if the pub was taken from her, this might be her best opportunity to taste the bread of ancient Egyptians. One she wanted to share with Graham.

Traditionally baked in a large ceramic pot over open flames, she planned to use the old brick oven set into the inglenook—the closest to a clay oven that she could manage in the heart of London. But today, she didn't have the patience, and perhaps not the time, to build a fire to raise the bricks to a high enough temperature. With a poker, she stirred the coals inside her modern cast iron stove back to life, added a few more, then pulled the teakettle into place, heating the water for tea.

A few moments later she was back at her worktable dividing the ancient sourdough culture in half.

Half she carefully fed—as instructed by Sēṇu māte—and set aside in reserve.

The remaining portion she dropped into a mixing bowl, adding water, emmer flour and salt. A simple basic recipe for flatbread, the kind the ancient Egyptians would have eaten, one that wouldn't detract from the flavor of the starter culture. Then she began to knead.

Graham stood in the doorway, a quizzical and amused look upon his face. "Do you often disrobe to bake in your corset?" he teased. "Here I thought your haste was to—"

"Oh, it is." She tossed him a flirty glance over her shoulder, one that invited him closer. "The sooner I set this dough aside to proof, the sooner we can—"

"Play?" His hands fell at her waistband atop the hooks and eyes that held it tight. Close, his hard body bumped against her soft backside. He spoke in a low voice that sent shivers down her spine. "I'd hate to see you overheat, what with a fire blazing in a nearby oven. Much as I approve of this baking attire, we can do better."

"We?"

"As your assistant, I'd advise we take further precautions."

"Oh?" Her voice suggested doubt even as his words stole the oxygen from the air. She dragged in a shallow breath. "Such as?"

"For example, with the temperature rising, a corset might prove too much."

"Is that so?" To issue a challenge, one he couldn't resist, she injected a note of doubt into the words, then sprinkled a handful of flour atop the wet dough and resumed kneading as if unconvinced. A game they'd played before. "I invite you to improve our working conditions as you see fit."

"Promoted so soon?" There was a tug at her waist. A pull. Anticipation sent her heart thumping and threatened to steal her focus from the bread beneath her hands. "Then I'd best earn my keep."

His fingers flew and various fastenings loosened.

One by one, her overskirt, skirt, petticoats and bustle fell away. Until, fingers still sunk into the dense dough, she stood in the kitchen, wearing nothing but her corset, combinations and an apron.

"You, sir, are a decided distraction." If a welcome one.

"Am I to be sent away?"

"Never." But even as the word left her mouth, deep in her stomach apprehension flapped its wings.

What was she going to do with this man? She loved him, but committing to a marriage when her first one had barely ended? Too much uncertainty hung in the balance for her to make promises, ones that would bind her, bind him and risk breaking their hearts anew.

She needed time.

"Trouble concentrating?" Words he spoke against her bare shoulder before nibbling along her collarbone. He trailed kisses on the curve of her neck, then nipped at her earlobe.

Pulling her hands from the bowl, she draped a tea towel over its opening—always best not to overwork emmer wheat —and began to turn. "Graham—"

"No." Strong hands gripped her hips. "Stay as you are. Hands on the table."

All spoken in a tone that gathered heat low in her belly. Heat that quickly spread, leaving her aching with need. His voice, his every touch—however slight—sent flames racing across her skin. "We've never had an empty kitchen to ourselves. Lean forward. Don't deny me this."

His last words a plea as he smoothed hands over the boned cotton of her corset, before tugging the laces loose.

Could she let go of her worries, enjoy the moment? "We're alone, truly alone?"

He stepped close, pressing the hard length of his body fully against hers. "I threw the latch behind me. Checked every room, no matter how small. Save for us, the pub is empty." Words spoken against her ear. "That we might indulge a long-held fantasy of mine, one I never thought possible."

"A messy one in the kitchen?" An air of laughter flitted through her reply. A fine layer of flour dusted the tabletop, her apron. Dough clung to her fingers. How was this romantic?

"Exactly this one. The perfect setting for worshipping the goddess of ancient yeast and flour."

Words that squeezed her heart tight, then set it free to pump hot blood racing through her veins. A surprise, his fantasy. One fueled by recent interactions? She didn't intend to ask. Far be it from her to discourage such a creative imag-ination.

She threw herself into the role.

"Oh? You're confident of your ability to please a goddess?" She didn't doubt it. And had every intention of returning the favor.

"Very." His hand cupped her breast beneath the apron, beneath her corset. Nothing but the thinnest cotton layer lay beneath his thumb as it began to circle her nipple.

She dropped her head back against his shoulder on a groan, a sound that praised any and all gods and goddesses.

His other hand dug into the curve of her hip and pulled her hard against him. Behind her, he was fully dressed and equally aroused. She relished the press of brass buttons, the rasp of wool, the smoothness of leather. And beneath it all, hard planes of muscle shifted as he rocked his hips, echoing her own desperate need with his own.

"Graham." His name emerged as a breathless appeal as forgotten sensations broke free, cascading through her. Every nerve ending was impatient and greedy for his touch, throbbing and aching, the desire so poignant it bordered on pain. She both wanted him to speed up and slow down. Everything now while savoring each glorious sensation.

His fingers pinched her nipple and she gasped, arching her back as his other hand shifted, slipping across her lower abdomen, traveling ever lower until fingertips found the slit in her combinations.

"Mmm. So ready." He scraped his teeth across her collarbone. At her back, his heart pounded with abandon. His knee pushed her thighs wider, and his hand delved deeper, parting her folds and finding her slick. Slow strokes threatened to drive her mad.

Unable to hold still any longer, she lifted her arms overhead searching for a way to anchor herself as turbulent emotions tangled with erotic sensations. Fanning her flour-coated fingers across his neck, she grabbed hold and issued an order like a demanding, entitled goddess. "More."

"Yes, my lady." His fingers sank inside of her, giving her more but still not enough.

Turning her head, she nipped his earlobe. "The table."

"Or is it an altar?"

She liked the way that sounded. "One you may join me on, but only if you strip to your skin."

His fingers slid free, leaving her empty as they took up their new quest. He unhooked the front of her corset and tossed it aside. Then spun her about and divested her of the nuisance of her combinations.

"Your wish is my command." His hands, palms rough with delightful callouses, wrapped around her bare waist and dropped her onto the kitchen table. A replacement for the bowl of ancient dough, which he took up, moving it to rise in the warm, draft-free space beside the stove. A necessary step when attending to a kitchen goddess.

Naked but for her stockings and boots, she sat in a scatter of flour and yeast atop the old and scarred wooden table, admiring the planes and ridges of his body as he shed first his holster and weapon, then the layers of his clothes. More muscle than she remembered, hard won in the desert, no doubt, flexed and shifted beneath the dark scatter of chest hair. His leanness served to highlight and define every delightful detail of his body. Soon a pile of discarded clothing rested upon the floor, and her man stood in all his naked and rampant glory.

Hers. All hers.

His dark gaze locked with hers as he stepped forward, pushing her with a firm hand against her breastbone, a gentle insistence she stretch out upon the table beneath her.

"Am I the goddess or the offering?" she teased, falling back upon her elbows, unable to resist the sensual promise in his eyes.

"You're certainly not something I'll ever sacrifice again." He pushed between her knees and, without further preamble, thick fingers slid inside her to resume their mind-altering strokes. "You're my goddess, mine alone to worship."

With that, he bent forward and added his tongue to the sweet torture to drag forth her cries, ones that grew increasingly louder. His fingers curved, his pace increased, her breaths came faster matching the flex of her hips.

Flat on her back, her mind emptied of all reason, arms spread to grip the edges of the table as her pelvis rocked, she could do nothing but whimper and beg for more as her entire body clenched, helpless but to chase after the tightening, coiling sensation at her center. The rough wood beneath her was an anchor, a hard and still surface, one in direct contrast to Graham's ever-moving mouth and hands. His mouth pulled. His fingers pumped. Stroked.

Forgotten sensations built ever higher until they collapsed inward, pressing down upon her sensitive core a moment before exploding outward. An unintelligible yell tore from her throat as she climaxed and his hands slowed, easing her return to the mortal plane. Finally, she settled, sated yet still not satisfied.

She turned her head, admiring the man beside her, all hard muscle, his obvious need carefully held in check. That would not do. Not at all.

Catching her breath, or enough of it to speak a few words, she issued an order. "Join me."

CHAPTER THIRTEEN

Julia scooted sideways, patting the table. A motion that sent a cloud of flour swirling in the air. Slanting in from a high kitchen window, the afternoon light glanced off the airborne particles and scattered. A fitting mystical atmosphere to accompany dreams finally fulfilled.

He stroked the back of his hand over the side of her face. "So beautiful."

A gentle motion even as his body screamed with a desperate need to be inside her. It was pure agony, balancing on the edge of assured pleasure. Yet he denied himself a moment more, pulling hairpins free and flinging them away without care for nothing was more erotic than a view of Julia, naked, with the soft silk of her tresses spilled across her shoulders. His goddess, wild and free.

Fixing an image of this moment in his mind he levered

himself onto the table with one hand. Leaning, he touched his lips to hers.

A gentle kiss at first, one to draw her back to arousal. A brush of his fingers across the side of her breast, dipping at her waist, flaring outward until his palm shaped the curve of her hip. He parted her lips and delved inside, a deep kiss that spoke of an unabated and long-denied hunger. Waiting for her breath to catch, for her pulse to quicken.

There it was, a spark. A soft gasp and a sharp lean forward. She nipped the corner of his mouth and a bolt of lightning shot through him, stiffening him harder than he'd imagined possible. It had been so long. So very, very long.

A hard shove at his chest tore him away.

"On your back, sir, that I might take my pleasure again." Mischief danced in her eyes.

He complied, reclining upon a thin dusting of ancient wheat.

His heart pounded, enjoying how their positions, if not their roles, now reversed.

On all fours, she crawled over him, then sat back atop his thighs. Fingertips lightly brushing over the ridges of his abdomen, lower and lower until they wrapped about his cock with their demands, ones that drew a low hiss from his mouth and sent a shudder through his body. Slowly, firmly her hand slid down, then up. Over and again, sending his eyes rolling to the back of his head.

"Look at me." An order. A command. One he eagerly obeyed. What a sight she was to behold. Pert breasts, nipples hard with desire. "Control yourself."

His hips bucked. The mind was willing, if not the body. "Julia."

She released him. Cold, punishing air rushed in and he groaned. "Nothing quick, not after all this time."

Rising to her knees once more, she crawled up his body, nipping her way to his mouth. Gentle teeth nibbled the angle of his jaw then, finally, her mouth landed upon his. He speared his fingers into her hair, holding tight as he drew her tongue inside his mouth in a tangled dance of give and take that left both their chests heaving with spiking desire.

Her legs spread across his hips. Soft breasts and hard nipples pressed to his chest as her hand reached for him, positioning his tip at her entrance. Sinking down upon him, inch by tight, warm inch, until—

A groan tore from his throat as she lifted away, pushed upright and dropped hard, seating him deep within her body. For a moment she stilled. "So good. So right."

Her flashing eyes told him that she remembered how much he liked watching her ride him. Hard. Breasts bouncing. Then her hips were rocking and the beginnings of a climax coiled at the base of his spine, winding and twisting.

Teeth gritted, he held on through the slow and gentle movements until her breath came faster, sharper. Until she rose up ever so slightly upon her knees, then fell. The extra friction all but snapped his sanity.

"Please," she cried. "I need—"

He knew exactly what she wanted. Fingers flexing as they held onto her hips, he lifted her. A gap just wide enough for them to slam back into each other. All at an angle that let him hit the sweet spot deep inside her. Over and again he rose as she fell, rough thrusts and sharp drops. Friction at its finest.

Her head fell back, hair swaying as he pumped into her. Everything tightened, but he held on, waiting for her, but needing release. He bent his knees, driving upward with even more force. Faster and faster.

Until a cry ripped from her throat, his name riding upon it. "Graham!"

Only then did he slip the leash. Once, twice. A third time. Then he hurdled over the peak behind her, crashing into an orgasm that emptied his brain and wrapped him in bliss.

She collapsed atop him, limp and soft and sated.

Long moments passed as their hearts slowed, as air returned to their lungs and blood resumed its normal pace through arteries and veins.

Her flour-dusted fingers threaded into his hair. "We're a mess," she murmured against his chest.

"But a glorious, satisfied mess." He tightened his arms about her waist, not wanting this moment to end, but knowing it must. And soon. There was no telling how much time they would be granted before unwanted parties came knocking with updates and questions. "And so very right."

"It is." The words he wanted to hear, yet he sensed a *but*.

"I won't hold you back, Julia." Words he considered a binding promise. "There's nothing I want to see more than you chasing after your academic and culinary dreams."

She sighed, shifting. Climbing from atop his body and

stealing away her warmth as she slid, naked, from the table and set about retrieving her undergarments.

He pushed upright, hopped down. He ought to be the happiest of men, but the suspicion that she intended to turn him down wouldn't stop slithering about in the pit of his stomach. "Julia?"

Shivers ran across his skin as she caught his gaze. "I want to say yes, Graham, but I can't. Not yet. Too much is uncertain."

"When this is all behind—"

"Maybe not even then," she interrupted, pulling on her combinations, buttoning them. "It's only that I've never had complete control of my life. Others have always been prioritized, especially men, as I've planned my future."

Icy cold ran down his spine. "I won't—"

"Stifle me," she finished. "Or make unreasonable demands. I know. But I need time."

"Time."

She caught his hand, pressed his palm to her chest. "You're the one, the only man for me. It's not that I want another. I want you here by my side. But—"

"You won't sign a marriage certificate." Words that he had to force out, numb. He pulled away, let her hand fall. "We can't live together except as husband and wife. Events of today aside, it's too improper to continue this way. Our reputations would suffer. Again."

"Separate homes, the occasional sharing of beds?" She fastened petticoats about her waist.

He wanted more than occasional. He wanted to come

home to her every night, to fall asleep with his arms wrapped around her. To wake beside her. Or at least to the sounds—and smells—of her early morning baking.

But she wanted time. He could grant that. After all, he'd been back in London less than a full day.

"For how long?" he asked. He shrugged on his shirt, pulled on his trousers, waiting. Hastily dressed, he pulled on his holster and fixed his weapon in place.

She shook her head, reached for her skirt and bodice, ignoring her corset. "How can I possibly know?"

He inhaled, exhaled. Swallowed his disappointment. He loved her and only her. A year apart had changed nothing, until today when the world shifted on its axis. Greedily, he wanted to claim her as his. Publicly.

"Fine." Her request was fair and just. "A prolonged engagement?"

She sighed. "No, Graham. A widow is respected as her own entity. A bride-to-be is not. She's a possession, no matter what the law upholds. And you have my heart. The rest will come with time."

He caught her arm and tugged her close. "Might I ask, on bended knee, in a month's time?"

"You may." She dragged a fingertip from the notch of his neck to his waistband. "My answer will likely disappoint, but I trust you to keep trying."

Her words promised enough. For now. "I will."

Beside them, the teakettle began to hiss and whistle.

"Shall we partake of ancient bread with freshly brewed

tea while dissecting a mechanical insect upon the kitchen table?" she asked.

"And take a close look at the beading of those necklaces in search of hidden secrets?" He dropped a swift, hard kiss atop her lips. "How swiftly we move to desecrate your altar."

"Maybe next time we add a little honey into the mix." She laughed at his expression of pure lust and pushed a tea towel into his hand. "Work first, then we'll see about sweetening the pot."

CHAPTER FOURTEEN

While she rolled out two rounds of flat bread and slid them into the oven to bake—they would need only few minutes—Graham cleaned the kitchen table, wiping away evidence of their activities. An act that had felt truly pagan. Worshiping each other's bodies in a blissful reunion of souls.

She wasn't ready to entangle their lives with the harsh realities of legalities.

No matter how many times he knelt on bended knee, she would not accept until she was fully in control of her life, with every option examined and settled. Never again would she rush into binding agreements without a full and complete understanding of expectations and roles. With any other man, she'd have declined outright.

But even as her head nodded in agreement, her heart rebelled, crying out for what it had so long been denied.

Measuring tea into a pot, she thought of the three sisters,

goddesses, who had ripped their lives up and traveled to London from distant countries for a new beginning. While it often felt like she had deep roots here at The Monocled Raven, tangled as they were with her family's history, perhaps it was time to let go, to begin anew.

Why this pub and not another, one that would not burden her with the invisible weight and expectations of the past? Could she afford to sell The Monocled Raven and begin anew elsewhere in the city? Dedicate herself to opening a pub focused upon rescuing ancient gastronomic delights by bringing them to present-day London?

But she was putting the steam cart before the clockwork horse. First they needed to deal with Harlowe. Only with her name cleared could she look to the future.

She poured boiling water atop the leaves and set the teapot aside to steep.

"Is this safe enough?" Graham asked, his voice uncertain.

She turned to find he'd placed the clockwork scarab upon a tea tray, one with tall edges.

Still, she hesitated. The contraption contained powdered ergot. But moving into the public room, away from the scene of food production, meant giving up the bright afternoon light and the cozy comfort of the only space that had ever been uniquely hers. A touch of heat blossomed on her face. Theirs. For she would never again be able to look at this table without thinking about what they'd done today—or about what she hoped to do again soon.

"Work with great care. I've no interest in baking hallucinations into my bread."

Graham snorted and, while he lined up the rest of the stolen artifacts upon tea towels, she set the teapot on the tray, added two teacups, two plates and—after a moment's consideration to what the ancient Egyptians would have eaten with their flatbread—nestled a pot of honey and a bowl of dried dates among the china.

Opening the heavy oven door, she reached inside the oven with a pair of iron tongs and flipped the bread. A caramel-like scent floated upward upon the heated air. A heavenly aroma unlike anything she'd smelled before in her kitchen, one imparted by the yeast starter culture Graham had brought her, filled the air.

She smiled. At the gift and the bread they were about to share.

One more minute to toast to a golden brown.

She closed the oven door, hovering nearby. Flatbread baked quickly and could easily burn.

The decapitated head of the clockwork gwyllgi sat alongside numerous Egyptian pectorals collected from Marston's body and those of the other unfortunate attendees at the impromptu cult meeting.

"Not what you'd expect advanced technological innovations to look like," he mused aloud, pulling a folded leather case from his pocket. "But I suppose that is entirely the point. People instinctively avoid menacing jackals and black dogs, harbingers of death that they are." He opened the case, revealing a set of simple tools, ones he would use to perform a cursory examination. "As to the jewelry, it's a common enough adornment by those bitten by the Egyptomania bug and unlikely to draw too much attention."

"Unless paired with elaborate costumes designed to mimic ancient styles."

"There is that." Graham paused, tool in hand, to sniff the air. "Is that the bread? It smells... different."

"In a good way?" She slid her hand into a mitt, opened the oven door and pulled out the baking sheet. With her tongs, she flipped a round of bread onto each plate and carried the tray to the table.

"Very much so." His stomach rumbled. Grinning, he set aside the screwdriver to reach for a plate. "All that physical activity has left me hungry."

She laughed. "I can't say I much enjoyed racing over graveyard gravel, but you know how much I enjoy kitchen activities."

He nodded. "Those were particularly satisfying. It's as if the goddess herself has rewarded my efforts."

She swatted his arm and dropped onto a stool beside him to pour tea. "Try it first plain, then we can add honey."

Together they bit into the bread. Ancient grains paired with ancient yeast. Simple ingredients no longer simply obtained.

"Mmm." She closed her eyes as she chewed and swallowed, analyzing the flavor, the texture. "Sweeter than the sourdough my mother's starter produced."

"It's softer than I expected," Graham commented. "Almost a cakelike crumb."

"Emmer wheat is higher in proteins, lower in gluten,"

she told him. "Making it a soft dough, requiring more gentle kneading. It's not as smooth or as stretchable as modern wheat dough."

"Interesting."

In quiet comfort, they dipped the bread in honey, nibbled upon dried dates and sipped tea.

Who, beside herself, might be interested in such an experience?

If she sold the pub and moved her business closer to the British Museum, she might stand a chance of enticing academically curious customers. Who might, given the convenience of proximity, be enticed to return. To become regular patrons. With the right seating, might she be able to encourage them to ensconce themselves while writing monographs and manuscripts?

"I can see the wheels and cogs turning in your mind." He slipped a piece of honey-dipped bread past her lips and she nipped playfully at his fingertips. He grinned. "Making plans to market this new bread to your customers?"

"I am." She sighed, standing to clear away their dishes. "A problem, given I no longer have any. Even before, the Fleet Street crowd was never overly excited about my experimental drinks and dishes."

Graham began with the gwyllgi head.

Screws removed, he was able to lift away a metal section of the clockwork creature's head, revealing the retracted antenna. Wires ran every which way, connecting to one thing, then another.

"I was told the tethersync inquisitor was powered with

one of our British Markoid batteries, but seeing such with my own eyes?" He whistled, low and slow. "Small. Compact. There's theory and then there's reality." His eyes glazed over with wonder, and his next words held a note of awe. "That he was able to pack so much circuitry into such a restricted space..."

A lock of hair fell across his forehead, reminding her of all the times she'd watched him, bed-rumpled, working at his desk in the early morning light, scribbling as he reworked mathematical equations to improve the function of his XRF analyzer.

"Can you explain?" Technology was not at all her forte.

He blinked and nodded, once again present and focused. "We gave the Ptah Institute the proprietary plans for our Markoid batteries, ones developed at the Rankine Institute, a gesture of good will and scientific exchange. In return, they agreed to share the plans for any development of a mobile signaling device—the inquisitor—that could contact a small mobile clockwork contraption."

"Like a skeet pigeon." She nodded. "But?"

"The ability to operate devices from a distance continues to be a nagging issue. Hence the retractable antennae powered by the Markoid battery..." He tapped a finger upon the table, thinking. "Even with those components in place, its maximum range, assuming no interference, would only be about fifty feet. If a building, a vehicle or trees fall between the inquisitor and its syntholink, all communication is lost, except—"

She brightened. "A problem solved by installing the

signaling device, this inquisitor, inside a swift four-footed mobile clockwork gwyllgi."

He drew breath, but she lifted a finger. "However, these are known components, if novel ones, that allow the clockwork insect and the four-footed hound to call and respond. How the scarab recognizes its targets remains an unknown, technology you believe the Bedouin developed and implemented to his financial gain."

"Precisely." He beamed as if she'd just solved a complex calculus equation.

"While my interests lie inside the mechanical beetle," he waved his hand at his tools, "I need you to examine the interior. If you'd care to place our specimen upon your tea tray, we'll take a closer look."

Opening the wire door of the birdcage, she assured herself that the switch remained in the "off" option, then placed the scarab with its mushroom-dotted carapace carefully before them.

Graham handed her a magnifying glass. "If our resident mycologist will take a second, closer look and begin to form conclusions before we begin the dissection."

"Thank you." She bent over the contraption, using a blunt-nosed probe to push at the bell-shaped caps of the tiny white mushrooms that had sprouted through the perforations in the contraption's elytron, the hard coverings that protected the wings. "*Mycena stylobates*, the bulbous bonnet, as confirmed in Sēṇu māte's workroom. Common. Inedible. Yet nonpoisonous. Which begs the question, why has its presence been carefully cultivated?"

"While our ergot mycotoxin lies within." Tiny brass screws fell, one by one, onto the tea towel. A few silver clips followed. Gripping the edges of the brass and blue faience carapace, he lifted it free and turned it over, pulling with it a webbed tissue not unlike a dense spider web. "Disgusting."

"It is not," she objected. "That is a mycelium. Merely the vegetative out-growth of the fungus. Rootlike structures, if you will. A structure that can convert biomass into energy into a carbon source, into a fuel." She squinted, nudged at a brown substrate adhering to the underside of the carapace. "One which appears to be growing on a layer of crushed leaves."

"Decorative?" he asked.

"Doubtful." She too fished for a logical explanation and came up largely empty-handed. "But perhaps designed to provide camouflage for the scarab when not in direct control of its maker? Though why one would choose to pair a mush-room not typically found in Egypt with a clockwork contrap-tion modeled after a beetle not found in Europe." She shrugged. "Perhaps further examinations will reveal a purpose."

Setting it aside, he indicated the contents of the abdom-inal cavity where a number of dark, seed-shaped kernels rested. "And this?"

"Ergot sclerotium as expected," she confirmed. "Unsprouted. And this purplish-black powder? Ergot powder. Enough to poison a handful of men and women." The internal mechanics lay before her, easier to view, exposed as they were, than through an optical magnifier. "And the grinding mechanism?"

"Simple enough," he said. "Insert the dried ergot, activate the clockwork mechanisms. The inner workings mill the ergot into a fine powder, then," he pointed, "this small belt conveys the resulting powder forward to the creature's mouth parts."

"Giving us The Kiss of the Scarab."

"The only question remaining is: did the clockwork scarab target specific victims last night? If so, how?" He lifted the magnifying glass, probing the insect's interior. "This is the syntholink, the latent transponder, that responded to the gwyllgi." He pointed with the tip of the probe to a structure inside the creature's abdomen. "Meaning this little wired tangle is our mystery device, the unknown piece of technology in play."

Eyebrows raised, she nudged his shoulder, letting a teasing lilt enter her voice. "You don't know what it is? Too much time in the world of archaeology, not enough time keeping up with the latest developments in the field?"

He snorted. "Nothing published matches this little beauty, or I'd have heard about it. Hence the word 'experimental'."

She lifted the pectoral taken from around her dead husband's neck and turned it over in her hands, examining every bead. "It must communicate with something in the necklaces, something that attracts the clockwork scarab." Playfully, she reached out a hand and ruffled his hair. "Such as 'screaming rocks'."

CHAPTER FIFTEEN

"Magnets," he agreed. The image of an iron bar wrapped with wire sprang to mind. Wire with an electrical current. Were rocks alive, he supposed it could be considered a tortuous procedure. But as it was impossible to give any credence to the idea of rocks in possession of emotions or feelings, no matter what this earth goddess may have claimed, he dismissed the notion. "Not that I'm aware of the ancient Egyptians using magnetite in their jewelry."

"Nothing looks unusual or out of place," she declared, passing him the pectoral. "No metal beads, at least not in this one." She swept her gaze over the other pectorals. "Or the others."

"Only iron, nickel or cobalt would be magnetic." He turned the necklace over in his hands, examining the gold sheet inlaid with semi-precious stones of carnelian, lapis lazuli and turquoise, checking each amulet and bead that had been strung together to form the intricate necklace. "Agreed. None of those appear to be present, at least nothing jumps out at me."

"Jumps." She held up a finger. With four quick steps, she crossed to the stove and returned with a pair of iron tongs. "If we're looking for a magnet, but gold, silver, and faience can't be magnetized…"

Such quick and clear thinking, seconds ahead of him. Was it any wonder he was enamored?

He spread the necklace out atop the table. Holding the tongs just above the pectoral, she passed the tongs over the beads.

Several beds lifted from the table, drawn to the iron of the kitchen tool, but one particularly large blue faience bead jumped upward and stuck tight. "I do believe we've found our 'screaming rocks'."

"Clever, hiding magnets inside perfectly ordinary-appearing beads." Graham grinned. "Always a pleasure working alongside a woman with such a sharp mind."

She beamed but stayed his hand as he reached for a pair of pliers. "Careful. If someone inserted a magnet, the beads are already damaged."

Faience, a fine powder of silica, lime, metallic colorants, and flux, left the outer surface of the material glazed, but the inner portion friable and porous. She was correct. Formed of composite material as it was, the bead might well disintegrate in their hands. He ought to know, having worked with the ceramic, both ancient and modern forms, during his attempts to use his XRF analyzer to study the causes of decay and deterioration of ancient faience found among and within ancient Egyptian burials.

"You're right." He set the elaborate pectoral aside. "Marston's dramatic death as leader of last night's gathering and as your former husband means we ought to save the reveal of any hidden contents, preserve the evidence, for when we have official witnesses present."

"This piece is less spectacular." She pulled one of the smaller pectorals forward, the one removed from the neck of the woman who had called for help, handing him the piece. "And the witness survived. She'll be able to testify, eventually, about the events of the evening."

"A good idea," he agreed. With the sweep of the tongs, another magnetic faience bead jumped upward. But only one.

"Interesting," she said. "Could the necklace with the most magnets determine the prime target?"

"It very well might." He scanned the other pectorals, those worn by the guests. "Only one bead per necklace is magnetic. Quantity might well be the determining factor."

He picked up their witness's pectoral. "Let's look inside." Gently, he gripped the spotted blue bead with his pliers. Sliding the pointed, needlelike tips of a pair of tweezers inside the bead alongside the string, he prodded, testing the innards. Small grains of mortar—the binding agent—fell onto the table.

"Anything?"

"Something is shifting," he said, trying to grip what felt like a smaller bead within.

Long seconds ticked past as she waited, her eyes on the bead's opening. A crack formed.

"Careful," Julia warned as a blue-green faience chip snapped free leaving behind a jagged edge.

Much as he agreed with her cautious approach, they needed to know what—exactly—they'd found.

"Almost there." He tugged and pulled, wiggling free a small grey-black tubular structure.

Before it could fall to the table, perchance to roll away, she held out the tongs.

Ping. The bead leapt to their surface and stuck tight.

"Clever." Graham tipped his head, considering the implications of their discovery. "Using a magnetic field hidden inside jewelry to mark a target." He snatched up the magnifying glass and bent over the clockwork scarab, focusing once again upon the small coils and loops of wire he'd found tucked deep within the insect's abdomen. Could it be? He suspected so. "I believe our talented Bedouin designed a miniaturized magnetometer." He straightened upon his stool. "What we have before us are the makings of an independent targeting system. Impressive."

"Terrifying is what it is," Julia countered on a huff. "Jewelry only marks the beginning of what individuals with nefarious intent might use this to accomplish. It's entirely too easy to slip such a small magnet into a pocket, into the lining of a coat. Tuck it inside the knot of a bow and a milliner or dressmaker could affix it to a hat, a dress, parasols, fans. The list is endless!" Her back was ramrod straight with indignation and righteous anger. "If such a thing as a tiny magnet can be used for murder and mayhem, it cannot be allowed to fall into the wrong hands."

"You're not wrong." He held up a finger, somewhat less concerned. "But with a magnet of this size, despite its strong pull, the clockwork scarab would need to be very close to detect its presence."

Somewhat mollified, Julia exhaled relief. "It would explain why you were always chasing after small cult gatherings, why the beetle didn't cut a wider swathe across the continent."

"So it would." He stared at the scatter of ancient artifacts and modern technology before him. "Save a magnetometer is not passive. It requires a power source," he squinted, once again leaning over the scarab, "and I don't see one. The Ptah Institute scientists developed a battery-powered tethersync inquisitor to interact with a passive transponder, the syntholink. That is part one of our known technological innovation here, the ability of the gwyllgi to signal the scarab, calling it to return, enabling whoever—"

"Harlowe," she prompted.

"Enabling first the Bedouin, then Harlowe, to retrieve the clockwork contraption once it was done with its assigned task."

She glowered. "Poisoning—kissing—those wearing one of these modified Egyptian pectorals."

His mind flew to the gift Marston had bestowed upon her last evening. "Do you think the professor meant to collect you before he departed for the cemetery?" But even as he spoke the question aloud, they were both shaking their heads. The man wasn't—hadn't been—of the forgetful academic variety.

"No." Her gaze slid away. "He was very clear about me waiting for him in my bedroom."

"Harlowe," he said simply. "It has his signature written all over it. Did he convince Marston to leave you behind or not?"

Had Marston objected to his wife's presence, embarrassed by the role he would play in the hope of revived virility, expecting Julia to be waiting for him at home in a warm, comfortable bed? Pliant and biddable upon his return. Or had Harlowe acted to keep Julia safe, that he might later claim the widow as his own? Pick up where his mentor left off? As a husband. As a proprietor of a pub. And owner of an antiquities dealership. He rather suspected so.

What, if any, were the limits of his ego? Did he also think to supplant Marston as Director of the Egyptology Department?

Wrenching his mind back from the cynical thoughts about the two men, he returned the entirety of his focus to the mechanics before him, frowning.

"There's only one problem. Part two. The interaction between the clockwork scarab and the magnetically charged beads."

"A power source," she said.

He nodded. "The only battery we've found is in the gwyllgi. There's nothing inside this scarab that could provide an electrical current to run the magnetometer." A frown carved itself into his face as he probed the contraption's inner workings. "At least, not one that I can detect."

What was he missing? What couldn't he see?

"The sprouting mushrooms!" Julia jumped to her feet, laughing at his puzzled expression. "The bulbous bonnet and its mycelial network. What pure, unadulterated brilliance!"

"You'll need to explain." Her comment left him at a loss, if amused. His first instinct was to deny that mushrooms could possibly have anything to do with this technology, yet there they were, growing through the perforated copper of the clockwork insect's back. Placed there purposefully. His eyebrows drew together. "Do you mean to tell me, they somehow produce energy?"

"Biological energy." She bounced on her toes. "Fungi can transmit small, albeit weak, electrical impulses—signals—along their rootlike hyphae. Perhaps it's acting as a battery to power your magnet-sensing device."

"Magnetometer," he supplied.

She nodded. "That. Whilst also allowing the clockwork insect to hide in leaf litter, concealing itself until called forth by the gwyllgi."

"Mechanical mysteries solved?" Amazed, he pondered the possibility. A fusion of biology and technology? An unusual intersection. "If so, this represents an enormous breakthrough." He spoke slowly, each word weighed down by heavy thoughts. "Why would the Bedouin pack it all into something as nonsensical as Egyptian antiquities and

Egyptian clockwork only to haul it north to Britain, to sell the lot to the likes of Marston?"

"The mushrooms," Julia reminded him. "The scientist's creation is fueled by a species not native to his homeland. *Mycena stylobates* prefers a warm, wet environment. Egypt is not particularly—or at least uniformly—wet." She tapped her chin, turning the problem over in her mind. "Perhaps he encountered extreme pressure to perform, but the only solutions presenting themselves would be unacceptable to his supervisors?"

"You think he packed up his—government funded—research and ran north, hoping to begin anew somewhere else?" He found himself nodding, academic theft was a possibility. It happened, if usually in a much more covert manner.

"Not exactly." She stretched out the words. "He's guilty of many underhanded deeds. Joining his improvised Order of the Winged Scarab was not free of charge. Fleecing the wealthy, leaving behind dead individuals, others with possible long-term health problems."

"Amassing as much wealth as he could along the way."

"Before selling it to a British buyer at a steep price, one convinced he could use the technology to augment his antiquities business?" She hesitated. "Marston crossed many lines into the gray, but openly breaking the law by purchasing a foreign government's classified technology?" She cringed. "I'm not convinced."

"You think Harlowe orchestrated the deal, concealing key information from his employer?" He was inclined to agree.

"It would explain why the inquisitor was inside his black dog, the gwyllgi," she said. "His obsession with druids moving to a new level. 'Harbinger of death.' What better way to hide stolen technology but to repackage it in another form?"

"One that could be kept on the move during our investigation."

"Save you caught it." She smiled. "Quite likely saving future lives. Harlowe may well have had plans to pay the Bedouin to repackage the technology in more Celtic forms."

"Thwarted," he agreed. "That's quite a lot of money invested. The Bedouin's technology would not have come cheap."

"Nor the Romani's work to produce the gwyllgi," she added. "Such illegal work cannot be sourced on Clockwork Corridor."

"And yet, you mentioned the pub has been running in the red."

She nodded. "Marston refused to reinvest any money in the business. All but the barest of our funds." She glanced at the door. "Yet the storeroom is filled with antiquities from the recent shipment. Most of them as-yet unspoken for. But they were all delivered long before the collection of pectorals arrived. With all our free cash tied up in questionable wares, what collateral would Marston have used as payment?"

He thought back to Harlowe's apartments. Comfortable, if spare. Had he amassed a stockpile of wealth, then invested it in a bid to take over Marston's position? "You think Harlowe used his own money to pay the Bedouin."

"It makes sense," she pointed out. "Marston died, hallu-cinating. Harlowe set him up, avoiding the cult gathering and carefully alibied himself."

"Which means any additional pectorals—"

"Or scarabs."

"Or scarabs," he repeated, nodding, "will be stored here, on the premises."

She bent, retrieving her ring of keys from the pile of discarded clothing, and separated one from the rest. "Would you like to begin a search of the storeroom while I," she swept a hand down her loose, flour-dusted clothing, "freshen up?"

Standing, he took the key from her hand. "We'll need to summon Black here, present our evidence." He brushed a lock of hair from her face, letting the backs of his knuckles trail across the side of her face. "Much as I enjoy the sight before me..."

"We should attend to appearances." She laughed softly, her cheeks flushing. "I won't be long."

"I'd be curious," he added, "to examine the pectoral given to you." If it contained more than one magnetic bead, he'd be sorely tempted to bring the man's life to an end at first opportunity.

"As would I." A frown tugged at her mouth. "It might shed light onto what Harlowe's plans were for me. I'll fetch it while I change." Gathering her corset and a few other items, Julia hurried up the back staircase that led to the owner's quarters above.

Key in hand, he headed for the hallway and the storeroom wondering how many additional magnetized pectorals he might find. Had disposing of Marston been his sole goal? Or had Harlowe held back a few of the necklaces in case a few other individuals became an inconvenient, if gullible, obstacle?

CHAPTER SIXTEEN

Julia threw her corset, stockings, and other assorted items on her bed, and glared at the winged scarab pectoral that sat, abandoned, atop her bedside table. How many magnetized beads would she find? None? Marking her as "to be preserved". One? Meaning Harlowe only hoped she would suffer the mildest of hallucinations. Or would there be an entire string of beads? That would certainly put a nail in the coffin, informing her of the man's true feelings toward her.

But even as she'd floated such possibilities, a new one had risen to the surface. One that made her break out in a cold sweat. Her own individual value aside, why else would Marston and/or Harlowe ship stolen foreign government technology across multiple international borders, technology that they'd immediately sold and employed?

Such illegal deals came with a steep price tag. Funds she doubted Marston possessed, unless...

If any immediate answers were to be found, they would be in her husband's room, tucked away inside the wall safe that was hidden behind an innocuous oil landscape.

She crossed the hall and lifted the painting away.

Both her father and Marston would have been surprised to learn she knew the code.

But as the eldest and presumed heir, Mother had instructed her, not merely in kitchen tasks, but in all things business. Though they'd been accompanied by a whisper, "Don't tell your father."

She dialed the combination as ice crystalized along her spine.

Before the Married Woman's Property Act of 1870, all property owned or inherited by a woman became the property of her husband. The new law hadn't sat well with Papa, who favored the old ways. Which was how she'd ended up in this mess. He'd insisted upon passing ownership of The Monocled Raven directly to Marston the day of their wedding.

She'd objected. Vociferously. But Papa was unbending and her sisters unsupportive. "It's the only offer you've got," one sister had snapped. "Marry him or we're all off to the poor house."

And so she had, but not until there'd been a written agreement that the pub would pass to her in the event of her husband's death. She'd read every last line. Twice.

However, such legal paperwork, no matter how binding, would have prevented Marston from mortgaging the property or—*aether forbid*—selling it.

A lump formed in her throat and her hands shook as she opened the safe and rifled through papers. Was that what she had witnessed the other night as she wiped counters and dried tankards? Marston selling Harlowe the pub in exchange for the funds to buy the clockwork scarab and its accompanying pectorals? Had his protégé conveniently neglected to mention the existence of the clockwork jackal, planning to retrieve the scarab after the event to hide all evidence of wrongdoing?

She rather thought it so.

Grabbing the entire stack of documents, she threw them atop Marston's bed. She spread them out, searching through the papers all while a growing panic consumed her.

"It's that one, on your right." Harlowe stood in the door-way. Smiling. A gun in his hand. With its muzzle pointed at her. "Congratulations, you figured out my plan."

She froze. Graham had searched the entire building and declared it empty. "How—"

"Did I gain access with those men guarding the pub?" Harlowe snorted. "The rooftop garden, of course. Where I keep my bee skep? No one ever remembers to look up. It's London. The buildings are so very close together. Sweet talk your way onto one roof, and the entirety of the city stretches before you."

And she and Graham had been distracted. Any overhead noise unnoticed as a traitor crept into their midst.

Harlowe gestured with the pistol. "Go ahead, take a look at the documents. Confirm what you suspect. You always were a bright one."

The lump of dread in her throat fell to her stomach, cold and hard and heavy.

She snatched up the paper, scanned the document. "Marston sold my pub." The words emerged from her mouth infused with such anger they were a foul curse. The edge of the document crumpled in her fist.

"*His* pub." Harlowe lifted a shoulder. "And everything was coming up glowing mushrooms until Leyton decided to stick his nose into my business. It could have been *our* business. Still could." He tipped his head. "Though I find myself having second thoughts given your recent amorous activities. The kitchen table, Julia?" He smirked. "Really? It's not at all sanitary."

"You watched?" Horror sent a hot flush across her face.

"My pub. My kitchen. My table." He waggled his eyebrows. "Hearing you cry out was quite arousing. Which is the only reason that I'm prepared to offer one last chance. Send Leyton away, marry me. We'll run the business together. I won't cut you out like Marston did."

She gaped. Was he delusional? Even if he believed he could avoid the charge of murder, the Queen's agents would pin international espionage charges upon him. At the very least, he was headed to prison.

How would marriage solve anything for him? Ah, he must be counting upon her silence. Spousal privilege would mean she could not be compelled to testify against him.

"All decisions regarding the pub will be yours," he continued, mistaking her silence as favorable contemplation of his offer. His arm lowered, pointing the muzzle at the floor as he took a step forward, a confident smile spread across his face. "If you want to use half the profit experimenting on bread and beer, I'll not stop you."

She stepped back. Away from his insanity. Then inwardly cursed herself. She ought to have held her ground, not shown any fear or reluctance. Now he was cognizant of the fact that she did not approve of his plans.

"Better if I pack my bag and cede the premises to you." Tossing the treacherous document atop the others, she managed to advance all of three feet before he stopped her.

"No." His arm snaked about her waist and spun her about. The muzzle of his gun pressed into her lower back.

She froze. "Reed—"

"Buttering me up by using my first name?" He laughed. His breath, hot and repulsive, brushed across her neck. "It won't work. You're not leaving with anything that's inside this building. As Marston's widow, you have many debts to pay, and I will collect what's owed me. I own everything. Every yeast you've nurtured—beer or bread—and every mushroom you've tucked among the green fronds of moss and ferns or beneath the tiny trees of your terrariums. Including those you gathered today. They're mine."

Digging deep and summoning every ounce of bravery, she attempted to bargain. "At least permit Leyton to leave." How had she managed to speak with much so confidence, without the slightest tremble to betray the fear churning inside her?

"No." An answer as cold and unforgiving as the steel of the gun. His fingers found the gap between her corset cover and her skirts, stroked over the soft skin at her waist, reminding her both of her vulnerability to a bullet and his amorous intentions. "Impossible. Even if I believed you would pack a suitcase and never return, his presence complicates things. You made a grave mistake, Julia, cooperating with the Queen's agents. I'd thought better of you."

She stiffened her back and huffed, as if only annoyed with him. "Why wouldn't I? Did you not allow Marston to gift me one of those Egyptian pectorals? Strongly suggest that I ought to wander through a deserted cemetery at night? You wanted me accused of murder!" Her heart gave a great thud. "Or dead."

"Accused of murder? Yes. I tried to convince Marston to take you with him to the ceremony, but he refused. It took the promise of glowing fermentable fungi to finally dislodge you from this cursed pub. But dead?" His low laugh wrapped cold tendrils of fear about her throat, slowly tightening until she could barely breathe. "Not at all, Julia. I wanted you for myself. Your pectoral was genuine and unmodified. The matsutake mushrooms were to have been a delightful surprise, a unique engagement to begin our new life together."

"You've been planning this?" All this time, pretending friendship, tempting her with intellectual oddities, yet he'd only been intent upon making her his wife?

"For months." He pulled her backward, tight against his chest, his hips. "Your role was to be that of the victim, of a wife wronged. I would have rescued you from suspicion. I've all the evidence I need to prove Marston acted on his own.

At first, your association with the Queen's agents was a threat, but with Leyton involved?" He cackled. "Our rivalry is well known. I'll claim self-defense. Then, with Leyton out of the way, we'll be able to start fresh."

"Please don't," she begged, swallowing back fear as she stalled for time. Whatever Harlowe had planned for Graham it likely ended in death. He knew too much. "I won't—"

"Tell?" he finished with a derisive snort. "Your word is nothing but an empty, nonbinding promise. But we'll fix that." His arm fell away, but the gun dug deeper into her ribs. "Put this on."

His hand returned, this time holding aloft a Celtic torc. Not one with the traditional gap between stylized terminals, but one that was hinged. One with two thick, solid metal loops that, when closed, permitted a fastener to be inserted.

She took the heavy piece from him. "Are you collaring me?"

"It's for your protection," he replied. "Put it on. Now."

What choice did she have? She could scream. Try to break free and run for the stairs. Would Harlowe pull the trigger? Leave her bleeding on the floor while he took aim at Leyton? Likely. A tear welled in the corner of her eye as she pushed her neck through the opening.

"Close it."

The loops snapped together. A tiny scraping sound met her ears as he slipped something into the clasp. Followed by a snap. Her hands flew up to the back of her neck and landed upon a tiny padlock.

"It's iron," he informed her, then stepped away, releasing

her. "Magnetized iron, its resonance tuned to the sensors of a different clockwork insect: the druid's bee."

Fingers curled around the collar as if she might rip it off, she spun about and gaped. "Bees?"

He snorted. "We'll not be continuing with the Egyptian antiquities trade. Not with the Crown's eyes upon us. No, Julia, we'll be moving on to new and greater things."

"But the gwyllgi..."

His eyebrows lifted. "Did you think there was only one? I've my own gearsmith engineer in my employ and more than one black hound at my beck and call." He snorted. "Busy as a bee, I've been, building hives of all kinds. Those I've gathered about possess numerous skills. A Celtic burial mound will be discovered, just as soon as we can put this unpleasantness behind us. As my wife, you'll have my protection."

"I'm not marrying you." She glared at him through narrowed eyes.

"Not even to ensure your own survival?" His eyes danced with an unholy light. "We'll be leaving London, retiring to the Devon countryside where you can recover from the trauma of living under the thumb of a man who used his position of power and influence at the British Museum to purchase and import a foreign government's technology. As his unwitting assistant, I will return to London to assist as best I can to see the scarab and its inquisitor returned to the proper authorities."

She frowned. Harlowe might well manage to distance himself from the fatal outcome of the mummy unwrapping party, claim ignorance of the technology hidden within, painting Marston as a financially desperate man grasping at a chance to secure himself wealth and power.

If he managed to destroy the evidence in her kitchen, to —she swallowed—kill Graham, no indisputable proof would remain. She was the only suspect caught at the scene of the crime. All the shipping paperwork was in Marston's name. Her husband had sold those pectorals to those men and women, then hosted the unwrapping ceremony in the cemetery. The only evidence of Harlowe's guilt was circumstantial.

She eyed the pistol in his hand. Though Harlowe had yet to kill anyone directly, he was committed. Her obvious choices were limited. Stand by his side and spout lies to protect him. Or meet with an unfortunate and fatal accident.

Best to go along with his plans for now.

"And what will I be doing?" she asked.

He exhaled, his shoulders visibly relaxing. Though his expression suggested he remained suspicious, he was content enough with her compliance. "You will be operating a country pub, surrounded by my friends."

Watched and guarded, he meant. "Fermenting honey into mead," she added. "What of my studies here?"

"I'll bring your terrariums to you. Tend to them as you will. Brew beer. Bake bread. Work upon your monograph."

"Warm your bed?" A note of challenge shot through her voice. That would never happen.

"As a wife does." He leered. "Speaking of which." He reached into his breast pocket and tugged out a piece of paper. "If you wish to live, proceed slowly and quietly to your bedroom." He waved the pistol at the doorway. "We'll marry today so as to avail ourselves of the full protection of the law. The benefits of friends in high places means I've a special license, and your appearance requires repair."

"Less scullery maid taken by the lord in the storeroom and more captive bride?"

He growled. "If the apron fits..."

Cooperate. Comply. Consent.

None of that would be happening. But she turned and, with the gun's muzzle trained upon her back, made her way into the hallway, one steady step after another. Until she was only a few feet from the top of the steep winding stairs that led down into the kitchen.

She took a deep breath and prayed the bullet would miss.

"Graham!" she screamed as she launched herself at the steps. Low and horizontal, she catapulted herself, curling into a tight ball as she tumbled downward. As hips, ribs, elbows, and knees smacked against treads and risers.

Above her, Harlowe cursed.

She crashed into the wall, then hurled herself sideways onto the flagstone kitchen floor before scrambling to gain her feet. All while the leather of her would-be captor's shoes thudded down the stairwell, seconds behind.

CHAPTER SEVENTEEN

Graham muttered under his breath. Words and phrases like "stolen" and "belongs in a museum" fell from his lips as he flipped back the lid of one wooden crate after another. He'd located a number of items listed as among the stolen Egyptian items but found no more suspicious pectorals—not so much as a single magnetic bead —nor did he find any ergot grains or powder. Also missing were any additional clockwork scarabs or large four-footed canines capable of transporting one—with or without a concealed inquisitor.

A fact which left him inexplicably grumpy.

They'd recaptured the scarab with an intact syntholink. The inquisitor hidden inside the gwyllgi's head was undamaged as was the Markoid battery. Both the board of the Ptah Institute *and* of the Rankine Institute would be mollified by the return of their respective stolen technologies.

More, they'd uncovered the Bedouin's secret project: a

miniaturized magnetometer powered by tiny fungi, an innovation that he expected the Ptah Institute would claim as their own. The Rankine Institute would argue but have little ground to stand upon. Arguments he was glad weren't his to mediate.

What more he'd expected to find, exactly, he wasn't certain. Not when everything in this building legally belonged to Marston.

With a firm alibi, Harlowe need only hold his hands in the air and deny knowledge of the professor's wrongdoings. He'd denied ownership of the clockwork Anubis. Nor had he ever claimed ownership of the gwyllgi—interest in Celtic druidism wasn't enough to pin the crime upon him.

They had no hard evidence tying the man to last night's events in Highgate cemetery.

Hands fisted at his side, he paused, closed his eyes, and took a deep breath. Slowly he exhaled and opened his eyes. Harlowe, cocky bastard that he was, enjoyed hiding in plain sight. What wasn't he seeing inside this storeroom? He turned, looking past everything Egyptian, searching instead for—

There. A gnarled walking stick. Forgotten and abandoned in the corner? Or deliberately placed?

He climbed over boxes, moving deeper into the storeroom and grabbed a wooden staff of blonde, twisted ash. Three feet tall, it could pass for a walking cane. It could also be one of Harlowe's staffs, an affectation he'd adopted during his druidic phase, then abandoned. But why leave it here?

The crates he stood among were a different color, a

different wood. He pried one open. Tucked among a bed of straw lay three drinking horns, the lip of each adorned with Celtic knot engravings. He dug through the packing material and uncovered a shallow wooden bowl carved with oak leaves and acorns. At the very bottom, he found hand-forged iron knives and torcs.

That gave him pause. Iron torcs? That seemed... wrong. They were traditionally made of twisted gold, silver, or bronze. Easier that way, to bend and twist so that the wearer might remove them.

"Graham!" Julia yelled his name. A warning.

Safe as he'd believed them inside her pub, the fear in her voice informed him otherwise.

He turned and leapt over crates at full speed. He burst into the hallway and drew his weapon as he ran to the kitchen, exploding into the room only to skid to a sudden stop. Taking quick aim, he squeezed the trigger. And missed. By a hair's breadth.

Harlowe returned fire, and Graham sucked air between his teeth as the path of a bullet tore through his shirt sleeve and left a gouge in his upper arm. Not a miss, but not a direct hit.

"Fire again," Harlowe growled, pressing the muzzle of his pistol against the side of her head, "and there won't be a girl left to fight over."

Graham raised his hands, pointing his TTX pistol at the ceiling. Her safety eclipsed everything.

Frustration gnawed at him, nonetheless. His jaw tightened. But such was the cruel reality of facing an adversary with a more deadly weapon pointed at the woman you loved. Darts loaded with neurotoxin designed to stun rather than kill weren't much of a match when a single bullet to the brain meant instant death.

"Place your weapon on the ground and slide it to me." Harlowe's eyebrows rose, his haughty expression daring his enemy to refuse.

With no real choice left to him, Graham did as asked.

Only then did Harlowe lower his own gun, shoving Julia roughly aside. Far enough to scoop the TTX pistol from the ground.

Smirking, comfortable with the impression that he had the upper hand, Harlowe straightened. He glanced at the TTX pistol, pointed it at the wall and fired. Once, twice. The darts shot across the room in quick succession and stuck, impaled in plaster. He tossed aside the empty weapon, then raised his own, redirecting the muzzle at Graham. "A most unfortunate way for old friends to gather."

"How did you get past the guards?" he demanded.

"Via the rooftop garden," Julia volunteered. "He's been here the whole time."

Her face was flushed bright red and Graham felt steam build beneath his collar. Their private moment, forever tarnished.

"That's right, Leyton," Harlowe said. "Perhaps next time, she and I will trial the surface of the bar. After hours, of course."

"You've a deft hand with women who can be bought for the night," Graham taunted. A quick glance at Julia confirmed she was relatively unharmed, though a dark iron ring now encircled her neck. A disturbing sight. Whatever Harlowe's plan, he expected his former friend aimed to eliminate the competition, as he had Marston, in a most disquieting manner. One which would deflect all guilt and blame. An unfortunate choice made by the victim. An accident. Nothing more. "Not so much with coercion. Is armed violence really the druid way?"

"Or forced marriage?" Julia raised her chin and turned her head to meet Graham's gaze as she spoke. "He's had this planned for weeks. Months, even. Harlowe leveraged Marston's bad investment, convinced my husband to sell him *my* pub in exchange for his life savings."

Graham took little satisfaction in confirming his instincts. Harlowe wanted Julia for his own, both running *his* business and warming *his* bed.

"Such is the nature of commerce, my love." Harlowe only looked amused. The man had no shame. Not a trace of regret or remorse distorted his features. "You stay one step ahead or you fall behind. Negotiations on the black market seldom result in a fair exchange."

"Which includes directing a man's newfound purchasing power toward stolen international goods?" His words were laced with insult.

"It wasn't hard to convince him." Harlowe lifted a shoulder, smiled. "Such was already his habit."

"Perhaps so." He shifted on his feet, moving himself ever so slightly to his right. The knife block might be out of reach —if he lunged, Harlowe would fire—but the stovetop was close. The water was barely off its boil, still blisteringly hot. He might have but a single moment to gain the advantage. "But you might have turned him in and reaped the profits without risking everything."

"Marston in prison, his penniless wife forced to stand by his side while agents questioned my story and compared it to his?" Harlowe shook his head. "I think not. An entirely unsatisfying ending. Especially when a more swift and permanent solution presented itself." He gestured broadly. "The pub is mine. The antiquities are mine. And as soon as old friends finish catching up, I will make Julia mine as well."

He'd thought as much. Suppressing this worry, he maintained a façade of composure. Was Harlowe holding back only long enough to taunt him, to relish the opportunity to spill all to a man he'd already condemned? The man was fond of bragging.

All too aware that any sudden moves could be a fatal misstep, his mind raced as he considered the man's motives behind the delay. Harlowe was in possession of a revolver with multiple rounds. And he'd yet to fire more than one bullet. Why?

A bullet was a simple solution, but the men were old rivals. Julia need only accuse Harlowe and things would go badly for him.

Which meant he had something else planned for Graham's death. Something that would provide plausible deniability and plant seeds of doubt in the minds of the authorities.

"Who initiated contact? The Bedouin?" he asked.

He shifted right another few inches, pleased to see that Julia took advantage of Harlowe's distraction to pull her feet under her. He'd not go down without a fight, but any altercation he instigated would, unfortunately, also place her at risk.

"A mutual business associate reached out, letting me know of an opportunity unlike any other." Harlowe inflated like a balloon full of hot air, both self-important and defying anyone to challenge his business acumen. "Marston himself would have turned down his proposal, but the professor's mistake was assigning me to read and sort incoming proposals."

As suspected, their former mentor had no inkling that his subordinate had strung a target about his neck, one masquerading as an Egyptian pectoral, then pointed a deadly scarab in his direction.

"Whereupon you decided to branch out on your own?"

"Ignore such an exciting opportunity?" Harlowe scoffed. He took a few steps to the left, mirroring Graham's movement, letting him know his movements had not gone unobserved. "I think not. The Bedouin is a rich man now. Able to relocate wherever he will, to live in luxury or pursue his work. Perhaps both."

Graham tipped his head and let a smile stretch across his face. "Are you certain of that?" On stockinged feet, Julia crept toward a counter reaching for a rolling pin resting beside a tin of flour. "This Bedouin wouldn't, say, be in a French prison in Calais, after a debauched night made him miss the ferry the next morning?"

Dark fury slammed down over Harlowe's face. "Did he

speak?" He yelled the words, demanding an answer. His arm shook, a worrying prospect given the weapon he held.

He took several steps backward and to the right. Julia lifted the rolling pin and prepared to swing. "He will. But there's still time to turn yourself in, to twist the story of Marston's death into a 'most unfortunate accident'." He shrugged. "It might work."

"And give up Julia? Surrender to you? Absolutely not!" His face grew bright red as he shouted.

Thunk!

She brought the rolling pin down upon Harlowe's arm, sending the pistol flying from his hand. *Bang!* A shot rang out, shattering a ceramic bowl. The weapon landed on the flagstones and slid with a clatter beneath the heavy iron cookstove.

Dammit.

Graham grabbed the kettle from the stovetop and heaved it at Harlowe, running for the knife block and wrapping his fist about the handle of a knife before dropping into a crouch.

Harlowe howled, but hot water barely slowed him. He shoved Julia roughly aside, slamming her ribs into a counter as he reached for... a basket?

No.

For a straw bee skep, one decidedly out of place inside a kitchen.

It was a moment's oddity that seemed to slow time.

Harlowe's fingers fell upon the small straw loop woven into its top. But instead of lifting the basket, he twisted the handle. First in one direction. Then back. Each sharp movement elicited a click, a sound at odds with the material used.

With Julia bent over, working hard to draw breath, Graham was at the disadvantage, trying to defend her *and* incapacitate their enemy.

He lunged with the knife, but Harlowe was equally limber. A fact the man worked to his advantage, keeping the large, solid mass of the kitchen table between them as they jockeyed right and left while also defending the door that led to the taproom, trapping them in the kitchen.

All while a buzzing hum built inside the bee skep.

Louder.

And louder.

Until a metallic droning filled the air.

On pointed metal legs, a clockwork insect the size of his fist emerged from inside the bee skep, its bright copper body flashing in the sunlight. Tiny mushrooms—a familiar species—grew from a metal grid that covered its thorax. A long, sharp stinger protruded from its rear end.

It launched into the air on thin, translucent wings.

Shit. Knives would do him little good against the coming onslaught.

"Is that concern I see upon your face?" Harlowe laughed. "Insects. So small, yet so very alarming when gathered together en masse to defend their own."

Another bee followed. And another. One clockwork bee after another leapt off the counter and took flight, until the malevolent buzz of a dozen or more bees filled the air.

The only option for escape was to retreat up the stairs, to race for the rooftop.

"Run, Julia." He didn't dare turn, lest the creatures stab him in the back. Moving his knife to his left hand, he grabbed a spatula. He'd played badminton a time or two, but this took the game to a whole new level. Birdies lobbed from one side of the net to another were a much less daunting prospect than a dozen angry insects darting through three-dimensional space—left, right, up, down. Nor had the penalty for missing been quite so high. He'd be playing for his life. "Upstairs. Call the guards from a window."

"Run, Julia," Harlowe echoed in a mocking tone. "Do as I asked, make yourself presentable. We're keeping a vicar waiting. But do take a last look at your lover. My bees are armed with ergot mycotoxins suspended in solution, a touch of re-engineering to ensure a direct path into the bloodstream via a spring-loaded hypodermic needle. A few stings will leave him incoherent and raving. More than that?" Harlowe shrugged. "If he survives—well, that would be a disappointment. I'd have to send my engineers back to the drawing board. Regardless, we'll be rid of this third wheel."

"You've lost your mind, Harlowe!" Julia, now upright, swept up a piece of crockery, took aim at a bee and heaved, clipping a wing, but failing to knock the contraption from the air. "If you think I'll ever speak vows binding myself to you!"

The bees had flown randomly about the room, but now gathered together, forming a glinting swarm. Still too high to reach, they turned as one unit, all zeroing in upon him.

Not Julia.

Not Harlowe.

Him.

This was the death his former friend wished to bestow upon him. Prolonged and painful. Dramatic and deniable. But no one developed such a weapon to only use it—them?—once.

Harlowe needed to be stopped. Here. Now.

Unfortunately, Graham couldn't see a clear path forward to that end.

A shield. He needed a shield. He grabbed a pot lid, holding it before him as a makeshift shield and readied for an attack.

"Missing something?" Harlow tapped the iron torc that he wore about his neck. One identical to the one he'd placed around Julia's.

"You reversed the signal?" Instead of attracting the attention of a poisonous clockwork creature, the torcs repelled them. Keeping their wearers safe while directing the mechanicals to act in their defense.

"How clever of you to figure it out." Harlowe flashed a smug smile. "If a bit too late."

The swarm dove.

Graham cursed and swung. Missed. He swung again and hurled one of the clockwork creatures into the wall. One banged off the pot lid.

A plate soared through the air. Missed. Shattered upon the floor. Another launched right behind the first as Julia raided the cupboard for ammunition.

All while Harlowe laughed and laughed.

CHAPTER EIGHTEEN

This wasn't working. At best, five bees were out of commission and no longer a threat, buzzing and twitching upon the floor.

So, instead, Julia took aim at Harlowe. Plates, cutlery, sacks of flour and sugar. Anything and everything she could lift and heave. All save her terrariums and yeast cultures.

Hands held in front of his face, he yelled at her to stop.

Not a chance.

So far, Graham was holding his own. But for how long?

As she passed her modern, commercial kitchen assistants, she flipped switches, turning on the massive steam mixer, the one that could knead the dough for a dozen loaves of bread at a time. Then the blender, able to puree entire bushels of fruit—with or without the pits removed. And finally, the sausage grinder, capable of mincing the gristliest of meats. All while keeping up a steady barrage of kitchen implements. An extreme cacophony of clanking and clanging filled the air.

"Aim here!" she yelled at Graham.

Ping. Clang. Dong.

Catching her meaning, he began directing his swings. Mostly, the creatures bounced off his makeshift sword and shield, recovering to attack again. But one swing shot a clockwork bee into the blender, shredding it, if destroying the kitchen device in the process. All that mattered was that there was one less bee in the air.

She rushed at Harlowe. "Please!" she cried. "Stop the bees! I'll do whatever you want. Just stop the bees."

His arms wrapped about her. "A little too late to convince me of your loyalty, Julia. Unfortunately, today a Queen's agent dies during the course of his investigation."

"Ow!" A sharp shout from Graham, followed by a stream of curses. He'd been stung.

The tears that streamed down her face weren't feigned. "Please." She leaned back, tugging hard upon Harlowe's arms, shifting him off balance in her direction. "I'll cooperate. Choose any dress you want me to wear. We'll leave straight away."

He fell forward a few tentative steps.

Graham jerked, swatted a bee off his shoulder, then redoubled his efforts. It was all she could do to not look over her shoulder. How many times had he been stung? How potent a preparation had Harlowe's druids managed to compound? Had this mycotoxin concentration been tested? On a human?

She pulled again. "Please."

Though Harlowe narrowed his eyes at her, he let her tug him along. Stupid of him, but it was very much an indication of how badly he wished for her cooperation in the courtroom *and* the bedroom. She'd leverage whatever she could to save Graham, diabolical though her plan might be.

Clang! A bee hit the side of the meat grinder and fell. Sounds of rending metal and crunching components met her ears. Then squeals of mechanical protest as the device announced it was broken beyond all hope of repair.

"Not now." Harlowe's gaze narrowed with suspicion. "We stay until this is done. I want to lay eyes upon your lover's corpse." He started to pull away, freeing one arm from her grip.

That wasn't happening with angry bees still zipping through the air unchecked. Her solution was brutal, but she saw no alternatives. Still holding onto his arm, she yanked one more time. Hard. He'd not fall for her tricks again. This would be her last opportunity.

And so she twisted, pushing against his wrist as if she might throw his arm across the room. Though such was not her aim. The dough hook spinning inside the massive steel drum, however, was. At full speed, the mixer caught upon Harlowe's coat sleeve, twisting as it spun. At lightning speed. In the space of seconds, the wool was yanked down his arm, torn away. But that wasn't the end of it, not by a long shot. Before he could open his mouth to cry out, the hook was back, grabbing hold of his shirtsleeve and, this time, hauling the man's arm into its rotations.

Screaming, breaking bones and other softer but no less disturbing sounds added to the discordant noise that filled her kitchen. Though her stomach twisted and her heart all but stopped at the deliberate and traumatic injury she'd caused another, there was no time to think about what she'd done. She ripped the iron torc from Harlowe's neck and spun away, racing around the table to stand behind Graham. Aligning the opening of the torc with the back of his neck, she pushed.

Immediately the clockwork bees buzzed upward, lifting away from the man they'd been attacking. Not confused—they were, after all, mostly mechanical creatures—but recalculating, reading the magnetic fields around them and responding to preprogrammed commands. A swarm of the half-dozen insects that remained reformed, this time its artificial fury directed at the man who had fashioned himself as their lord and master.

Graham threw away the pot lid and spatula, gathering her close against his chest. "You can close your eyes."

A quiet suggestion, but not one she intended to follow. She swallowed and braced herself, letting him know with the smallest shake of her head that she would not look away from the final tragedy in the disaster of her kitchen.

Harlowe, his arm twisted and mangled into a bloody, unrecognizable mass slumped against her now broken and still mixer. He raised his head, glared at her and hissed, "There is no antidote. He dies with me."

Her heart stuttered at his words, but while he wasn't wrong, he wasn't necessarily right. The poison was in the dose. Trapped as Harlowe was, he was defenseless and open to attack. She cringed as the clockwork bees dove, stinging him repeatedly about the head and neck and shoulders.

In the distance, she heard pounding. Agents at the front door concerned at the clamor and uproar within.

"Help has arrived, if too little and too late."

"They can't be allowed in here," Graham said. "But I don't think I can reach the kitchen door." His knees gave out.

She caught him beneath his arms, helping ease him to the floor. Then she slammed the kitchen door closed and wedged a chair beneath the handle before dropping onto her knees beside him.

Brushing aside hair that had fallen across his forehead, she asked, "How many times were you stung? Where?" Her voice wavered with worry.

"Twice." He waved at his forearm, at his collarbone. "But only briefly. I've a touch of nausea and the tips of my fingers are oddly cold considering how fast my heart is racing. But no hallucinations."

There was nothing to be done to counteract the ergot alkaloids coursing through his system. Supportive hydration, rest, and time. Everything else was out of her hands.

Not that it stopped her from pushing back his shirt-sleeves or unbuttoning his collar, from shoving aside the ruin of his linen shirt to confirm the number of hypodermic needles that had pierced his skin. There was a little redness and he winced as she inspected each site but found no signif-icant damage.

Still, her stomach clenched with worry.

"Most likely due to vasoconstriction," she pronounced. She lowered her forehead to rest upon his shoulder. Mild effects so far. Odds were the clockwork insects had only managed to inject the tiniest of doses, that his symptoms would resolve in a few hours. But there was no way to know, no way to calculate the effects even if she knew the exact amount of toxin coursing through his veins and arteries. "The alkaloids are known to stop bleeding."

In small doses in targeted locations. Massive, over-whelming amounts, however... Well, the effects hadn't helped Harlowe. In the end, she wasn't certain what likely killed Harlowe first, blood loss from mechanical injury or the sudden and extreme vasoconstriction brought on by ergot poisoning.

The buzzing noise lessened. The clockwork bees, their abdomens presumably now empty of mycotoxins, wandered aimlessly atop her counters. Then one lifted into the air, circled the room twice, then returned to its beehive. One by one, the others followed suit.

Quiet, if not peace, descended upon them.

"You never answered me." Graham tipped up her chin with his fingertips, caught her gaze with his.

"Now?" She bit her lip. "You want an answer now, here? Amid this disaster?"

"Because you keep avoiding the question." He offered a smile, if a wistful one. "I'm in love with you, Julia." He stated the words slowly and clearly. "I want to marry you. Do you not return the sentiment, or—"

She pressed two fingertips to his lips. "It's not that." She took a deep breath and let words rush forth. "I love you. I want no other man in my life. I *do* want you by my side, always. But I've never had the freedom to control the direction of my future. I don't even now. Not only does The Monocled Raven not belong to me, its essence feels... desecrated. Haunted. By memories both good and bad. What I need is a fresh start, somewhere else."

"But not with *someone* else?" Worry crinkled his forehead.

"I'll marry you, Graham." Tears welled in her eyes as all the emotions of the day threatened to overwhelm. "I *want* to marry you and only you. But not yet. I need time to sort out the mess of my life, not to simply offload all of my problems onto you."

"Us," he corrected. He threaded his fingers through hers and squeezed. "We would solve them together."

"I know." She looked away, fighting the temptation of his words. It would be so very easy to lean on a man, especially one she loved so very much. "But I *want* to solve them myself, to come to you whole and not as a burden."

"Standing on your own two feet." His thumb stoked across her cheek.

Warmth spread through her chest. He understood.

"It might take some time," she said. "I'll accept the position at Oxford, work as a professor until I can afford to buy a new property—" She considered London prices. "Somewhere."

"No need." Graham was shaking his head. "Not unless that's what you really want to do. Ownership of this pub will be passed to you; Black will ensure the Crown agrees."

"He can do that?" Her heart leapt, stuttered.

"And more." The certainty in his words was reassuring. "You'll not be held responsible for Marston's wrongdoings, though the contents of your storage room will be confiscated, leaving you with little beyond the walls that surround us."

She nodded, the decision easy and obvious. "Then I'm selling the pub."

"Selling The Monocled Raven?" Doubt drew his eyebrows together. "After it's been in your family for generations?"

It stung a bit, she wouldn't deny it, but... "It's time for a fresh start. This kitchen is ruined. And the clientele? I could offer all the old favorite drinks and dishes, win them back, but what I'd really like is to begin anew. Elsewhere."

Worry crept across his face. "Not in Oxford, I hope?"

"No, here in London. I've no wish to leave the British Museum behind and, while this might make me sound insane, I'd love to open a pub that offers historical food and drink. To cater to the erudite as well as those who want nothing more than a traditional meal."

"That's a brilliant idea." His lips curved upward. "May I suggest one near the museum?"

"With accommodations above?" She returned his smile. "Will you help me look for properties?"

"I'd like nothing more. Will you decorate with collecting

baskets, mushroom-shaped lamps, logs for stools and benches?"

"With accents of moss and fern?" She laughed. "I just might."

Graham tipped up her chin with his fingertips and pressed a kiss to her lips. One that deepened in the most promising manner until fists pounded on the kitchen door.

"Open up!"

"Don't enter!" Graham shouted.

But there was no prolonging their moment.

"Agent Leyton?" the agent called back, clearly unconvinced.

Graham sighed. "They won't wait much longer, no matter what we say."

"I'll plug the hive." Reluctantly, Julia stood.

"Please wait!" she shouted at the wooden door. "It's not safe for you! Mr. Harlowe deployed a targeted clockwork weapon! We're safe but need a moment to be certain it's fully disabled!"

She hurried to the bee skep and stuffed a tea towel into its opening. A simple solution. She'd leave it to the Rankine engineers to take the risks of exploring the mechanics of the swarming insects and their home. With precautions in place, they would likely enjoy disassembling the unassuming wicker hive to examine all the mechanics, both stationary and mobile, concealed inside.

With that, she hauled away the chair and opened the door.

Weapons drawn, agents rushed into the room, then froze.

With no immediate action to take, they gaped at Harlowe's swollen, mangled body, averted their gaze from Julia, half-dressed and disheveled as she was, finally focusing upon Graham, equally unkempt.

One heaved a sigh. "Start talking."

EPILOGUE

Late Autumn, 1885

At last, she was his.

And he was hers.

Not without reluctance, Graham broke their kiss. Breathless, he locked eyes with his wife. He refused to look over his shoulder, where an entire pub full of well-wishers awaited. Family. Fellow agents. Engineers. Archaeologists. And none other than Sēṇu māte herself. If anyone wondered at the length of time their steam carriage had been stopped before The Wise Mushroom or why it was taking the bride and groom so long to join them, he didn't care.

Let them look. They were done hiding their feelings from the world.

Their lives had been a whirlwind these last few weeks and they deserved a few last moments alone.

For the last few weeks, Julia had worked at a furious

pace. Selling The Monocled Raven. Seeking out a likely property in Bloomsbury, a short walk from the British Museum. Overseeing endless renovations. All while she baked and brewed and fermented in the back rooms that served as both kitchens *and* laboratory. The ancient Egyptian flatbread on the menu had indeed drawn curious archeologists into her pub and her matsutake mushroom ale was a popular novelty, glowing faintly yellow as it did. Though he preferred not to think about how quickly the fungi or the pine sapling had grown under his wife's care, it was unavoidable. A mechanical engineer had been commissioned to construct a sturdy rooftop garden to support a small forest. Occasionally she fretted about the fairy ring, worried that it might one day encircle the entirety of the garden, though Sēṇu māte assured his wife that she would handle any uncanny side effects it might create.

Most everything in her pub was new. Save for the sturdy kitchen table. That, they'd agreed, moved with them to the new property.

While Julia's hands were full, he'd been busy establishing a laboratory at the Rankine Institute, preparatory to sharing research space with Sinan Nabil, an Egyptian scientist en route to work by his side. The clockwork bees and the skep held advanced electronics, the specifics of which they were set to tease out, to reverse engineer. There certainly wouldn't be any help from Harlowe's engineers. One by one, his "druids" had returned their magnetic iron torcs in the dark of night—a white flag?—before melting into the countryside, untraceable.

Though they had no immediate plans for a honeymoon, a Mesopotamian archaeologist had agreed to let them join his excavation team next season at Nineveh alongside the Tigris River. Julia would hunt through bakeries and breweries in search of new yeast. He would apply his XRF analyzer to study the alkaline-based flux of the early colored glazes used to decorate ceramics.

As he looked into Julia's eyes, a deep sense of contentment washed over him. He'd married the love of his life. His heart soared.

"Ready, Mrs. Leyton?" He tapped the brim of her bonnet, a small creation perched atop twists of dark hair. A red ribbon embroidered in a traditional Latvian pattern wrapped about its brim and was joined by a small cluster of ferns and moss and a gathering of small, brown mushrooms. Midst it all to commemorate their reunion, a tiny, winged scarab.

Sans clockwork.

"More than I can possibly articulate." She pressed the palm of her hand to the side of his face, her eyes shimmered, reflecting his own happiness and delight. "I've everything I could wish for, including a husband I love dearly. Carry me over the threshold?"

ABOUT THE AUTHOR

Though ANNE RENWICK holds a Ph.D. in biology and greatly enjoyed tormenting the overburdened undergraduates who were her students, fiction has always been her first love. Today, she writes steampunk romance, placing a new kind of biotech in the hands of mad scientists, proper young ladies and determined villains.

Anne brings an unusual perspective to steampunk. A number of years spent locked inside the bowels of a biological research facility left her permanently altered. In her steampunk world, the Victorian fascination with all things anatomical led to a number of alarming biotechnological advances. Ones that the enemies of Britain would dearly love to possess.

www.AnneRenwick.com

instagram.com/anne_renwick

facebook.com/AnneRenwickAuthor

pinterest.com/AuthorAnneRenwick

www.ingramcontent.com/pod-product-compliance
Lightning Source LLC
Chambersburg PA
CBHW061811190726
48289CB00007B/2157